E V E R Y
SHALLOW
CUT

TOM PICCIRILLI

ChiZine Publications

FIRST EDITION

Every Shallow Cut © 2011 by Tom Piccirilli
Cover artwork © 2011 by Erik Mohr
Cover design © 2011 by Corey Beep
All Rights Reserved.

LIBRARY AND ARCHIVES CANADA CATALOGUING IN PUBLICATION

Piccirilli, Tom
             Every shallow cut / Tom Piccirilli.

ISBN 978-1-926851-10-5

             I. Title.

PS3566.I266E84 2011   813'.54   C2010-907282-0

CHIZINE PUBLICATIONS
Toronto, Canada
www.chizinepub.com
info@chizinepub.com

Edited and copyedited by Brett Alexander Savory
Proofread by Samantha Beiko

Printed in Canada

For everyone with an unfulfilled hope, a mediocre dream, a half-forgotten love, a vague regret, a thorn of disappointment, an average fantasy, a fear of failure, a ghost that walks the midnight corridors, Every Shallow Cut *is for you—*

EVERY SHALLOW
SHALLOW
CUT

dreams. I was three days into my life as a homeless loser drifter when they broke my nose and dropped me on the street in front of a nameless pawn shop. I hit like two hundred pounds of failed dreams. I was three days into my life as a homeless loser drifter when they broke my nose and dropped me on the street in front of a nameless pawn shop. I hit like two hundred pounds of failed dreams. I was three days into my life as a homeless loser drifter when they broke my nose and dropped me on the street in front of a nameless pawn shop. I hit like two hundred pounds of failed dreams. I was three days into my life as a homeless loser drifter when they broke my nose and dropped me on the street in front of a nameless pawn shop. I hit like two hundred pounds of failed dreams. I was three days into my life as a homeless loser drifter when they broke my nose and dropped me on the street in front of a nameless pawn shop. I hit like two hundred pounds of failed dreams. I was three days into my life as a homeless loser drifter when they broke my nose and dropped me on the street in front of a nameless pawn shop. I hit like two hundred pounds of failed dreams. I was three days into my life as a homeless loser drifter when they broke my nose and dropped me on the street in front of a nameless pawn shop. I hit like two hundred pounds of failed dreams.

I was three days into my life as a homeless loser drifter when they broke my nose and dropped me on the street in front of a nameless pawn shop. I hit like two hundred pounds of failed dreams.

My gold band wedding ring was still on my finger, covered in spit, because I'd been trying to work it out of a ten-year groove in my flesh. My mother's beloved nineteenth-century art prints and my father's prized coin collection scattered across the cement. It's all I had left of my parents and all I had left of any value. Churchill barked like a state ward maniac, trying to work his snout through the three-inch space of open car window. He hadn't eaten today and sounded a little raw and weak.

I hadn't even gotten out of Denver yet. I'd been killing time the last few days, circling the city and doing my best not to puke at the thought of driving home to New York and showing up on my brother's doorstep. I knew how it would go down. He would give me the slow once-over. He would pull a face. He wouldn't give me a brotherly hug. He'd chuckle but it wouldn't be tinged with humour, it would be coming from a place behind his spleen where he kept all his self-righteousness. He'd point me to a guest room that would have a fruity air freshener plugged into the wall that spritzed the place down automatically every twenty minutes. It would smell like every funeral I'd ever been to. He'd feed me well and offer me money to help me get back on my feet. He'd set me up on dates with successful middle-aged women who would find my grey hair distinguished and cry in my arms after we made love. He'd hide his sneer and I'd do my best to be grateful until the day came when I went for his throat.

Churchill let loose with a howl. He missed his spot on the end of the futon. I missed my spot lying next to my wife on our king-size bed. I missed my house. The bank owned it now. I'd thought I'd put down some deep roots over the last ten years but they'd all been tugged up like a handful of dying weeds.

I had a final royalty cheque in my pocket for $12.37. For some reason I was hesitant to cash it. Maybe because it was the last money I'd ever see from my writing. My last novel had sold even worse than the one before it, which had sold worse than the one before that, going back more than a decade to the first book, which hadn't done all that well either.

Somehow though, I'd managed to swing the mortgage every month until the so-called economic crisis dovetailed perfectly with the self-destruction of my marriage. I still wasn't sure what had happened. It had all just fallen apart so slowly and steadily that I never noticed I was walking off the big ledge—until the creditors began repossessing my furniture and my wife started texting a guy she called "sweetie." Sweetie came by one day and helped her move all her belongings into the back of his 4 x 4 while I fielded calls from the mortgage company.

I turned over onto my back on the sidewalk in front of the pawn shop and someone kicked me in the ribs. My vision turned red at the edges and my head filled with the voice of my editor telling me I simply wasn't commercial enough. Readers wanted more mainstream material. They didn't want sentences that sounded like poetry. No one read poetry. No one liked poetry. This wasn't the fucking Renaissance.

I tried to tighten into a ball but the next kick caught me in the hinge of the jaw. I tasted blood. It was thick and probably full of sodium and fat or whatever else gave you arterial sclerosis. My old man's heart had given out on the job he'd put forty years into. My mother's heart had failed on her third night in the hospital for a varicose vein operation. My brother's pulse was as strong as a stallion's and he played tennis twice a week with the bluebloods on the bay.

Just for the fuck of it they stomped the prints. Someone went for my ring finger. I really hoped they didn't have wire cutters. They tugged and tugged until I thought my finger would break, but they quit before that. They scooped up the coins.

I couldn't tell how many of these punks there were. Three maybe, looked like your average hardass street trash. They went for my wallet. It made me snicker. What were they going to get there? I had eight bucks in cash and three maxed out credit cards. Good, they could steal them and deal with the bill collectors from now on.

My laughter pissed them off. They started to stomp me. It made me laugh louder. I hoped they would take the royalty cheque and forge my name and try to cash it. I wondered if they could handle the superior smarmy leers of the bank tellers who always gave me the fish eye when I brought in a cheque that small. When I needed to withdraw six bucks so I could put a couple gallons in the car. When I brought in my spare change and it added up to five bucks at a shot.

"This prick is crazy," one of them said.

I sipped air through the pain and clenched my eyes against the tears and wondered if Sweetie was a fan of chick flicks and vanilla incense.

Then they opened the car door and Churchill hit the ground beside me with a thirty-five pound belly-flop. Our gazes met and he gave me such a look of confusion and unconditional love that a sob welled in my chest and nearly broke from my throat. He snuffled at my neck and licked me twice and they went for the keys in my pocket and Churchill went for their ankles.

I had a flash, almost a premonition, where I saw that here it was, my very worst moment in a long chain of very worst moments, where I was going to have to watch them kick my dog to death. It was worse than my wife leaving me, it was worse than losing the house, it was worse than visiting the graves of my parents. It was going to be nearly as bad as the day I'd passed wailing protesters at Planned Parenthood following my wife's staunch shoulders across the lot. They'd break Churchill's back, boot him into the gutter, dance off with my father's coins, and drive away in my car.

Church growled and hung onto an ankle, and the guy tried to shake him and bitched, "Fucking fat dog piece of shit!" His partners found it funny and started to laugh. I got to my knees and then to my feet, and I remembered that I was a man with nothing left who wrote stories about men with nothing left who did ungodly acts of violence against each other.

I wrote from the safety of a desk but the dark cellar door of my failures had opened and called me through it, and I found all my urgent whispering pain and hate, and I laughed again and they turned to look at me and I went to work.

oressed harder. The mook folded in half and I kneed him in

t in my left hand and tightened my thumb down on his Adar

ne kind of sound that Church makes after eating too much

narder. The mook folded in half and I kneed him in the face.

left hand and tightened my thumb down on his Adam's

ind of sound that Church makes after eating too much chili o

The mook folded in half and I kneed him in the face. I gr

and and tightened my thumb down on his Adam's apple. He

nd that Church makes after eating too much chili con carne.

< folded in half and I kneed him in the face. I gripped his thr

ntened my thumb down on his Adam's apple. He made the s

urch makes after eating too much chili con carne. I presse

d in half and I kneed him in the face. I gripped his throat

ed my thumb down on his Adam's apple. He made the sam

ch makes after eating too much chili con carne. I pressed ha

alf and I kneed him in the face. I gripped his throat in my left

mb down on his Adam's apple. He made the same kind of s

ter eating too much chili con carne. I pressed harder. The mo

d him in the face. I gripped his throat in my left hand and

on his Adam's apple. He made the same kind of sound tha

ng too much chili con carne. I pressed harder. The mook

im in the face. I gripped his throat in my left hand and tigh

his Adam's apple. He made the same kind of sound that Chur

much chili con carne. I pressed harder. The mook folded in

e face. I gripped his throat in my left hand and tightened

is apple. He made the same kind of sound that Church m

chili con carne. I pressed harder. The mook folded in half and

pped his throat in my left hand and tightened his thumb

He made the same kind of sound that Church makes after

n carne. I pressed harder. The mook folded in half and I

ed his throat in my left hand and tightened his thumb

made the same kind of sound that Church makes after

much chili con carne. I pressed harder.

I'd lost eighty pounds of flab in the year since Sweetie had entered my life. I vomited more than I ate. A decade at a desk putting my guts on paper had made me obese, and the dissolution of my marriage and stress over a failed career had gnawed at me like cancer. But instead of being sick, I'd become healthy. Lean, trim, strong.

I was still trying to figure out how to use my new body. I moved swiftly in ways I didn't recall. My muscles were corded and black veins twisted along my wrists and forearms. I listened to Churchill snarling while I sucked down my own blood, grabbed the number three punk and hammered him under the heart with a hard right hook.

I hadn't thrown a punch since junior high when some kid hocked on an essay I'd spent three days writing. I still didn't know what that was all about, but I'd brought a wild roundhouse up from my knees that hadn't come within three inches of his chin. He beat the shit out of me. I suspected he had self-esteem issues. Now I had a few of my own.

I lashed out. I kept my hands up and elbows tight to my sides. I'd written a lot of tales of killers on the prowl, heroes defending their honeypies, champions who rose above ignorance and setback to win respect and true love. I wanted to kill the fuckers.

The blood kept pulsing down my throat. The taste reminded me of steak night at Jensen's in LoDo. You finish a sixty ouncer and it's free. Jensen had lost money on my fat ass. Black spots danced in front of my eyes. I twisted and brought an elbow back into the punk's teeth before the number two mook was on me.

My lips moved and a voice I didn't recognize

as my own said, "Oh yes." I didn't know to what it was referring. The mook had a bicycle chain wrapped around his knuckles. He was a kid, maybe twenty, wearing one of those knitted hats, baggy jeans, a wife-beater T. I thought he should be at home reading *Catcher in the Rye* or *Slaughterhouse-Five* or *On the Road*. He should be sending me emails about art and literature, and he should beg me to be his mentor. I'd critique his first fumbling steps into the writing world and we'd both suffer the vagaries of art together.

His heavy-lidded eyes held no spark. His face was scabbed over from picking at it so much because the meth had driven his nerves toward frenzy. He punched me in the centre of my chest and the pain fired up into my brain like a short fuse on a stick of sweating dynamite. I almost asked him to do it again.

I gripped his throat in my left hand and tightened my thumb down on his Adam's apple. He made the same kind of sound that Church makes after eating too much chili con carne. I pressed harder. The mook folded in half and I kneed him in the face.

I rushed across my mother's prints to the last punk, who was still trying to shake Churchill loose. I looked at my boy scrabbling for purchase on the cement and thought this was a lot like playing tug-of-war with him in our backyard at home. When we had a home. He looked happy. He looked like he could do this all day long.

The prick was reaching into his back pocket. I hesitated a second, wondering what he was going to pull. I'd written this same scene many times before. I knew the choreography as if we had practised and performed this ballet a thousand nights to raves across the world.

Church finally rolled free with a grunt. He flipped over hard and banged his chin on the curb and let out a yelp. For the first time I realized there were dozens of people lined up on both sides of the street watching. No one offered any help. I didn't see anyone holding a cell phone to their ear calling the cops. It felt like they were all just waiting their turn in line to get at me. An old man at the curb, a girl on a bike. I thought, You next. Then you. Then you. Then you.

The knife finally came out. The prick snapped it open and I noted it was a four-inch blade. I'd written before about knives like this going between ribs and up into the heart. I wondered if he had the skill to do it to me in just the right way. Get up behind me, yank my chin aside, expose the floating ribs, then up and twist. I wondered if I should offer him a clear shot at my left side. I wondered if he even knew that the human heart is on the left side of a man's chest.

He glanced down at his two buddies on the ground. His eyes shifted to my father's coins and he wet his lips. So did I. His gaze finally struck my face and I saw him frown, a bit puzzled now, like he hadn't seen me before, or I wasn't the person he was expecting. The knife wagged back and forth. He wasn't holding it right. He had it gripped in his fist, like he was going to draw it back over his head and plunge it down into a Thanksgiving turkey. I thought he should hand it over now and I'd show him how to grip it correctly. Hold it lightly across the second knuckles, low for easy slashing, stabbing, and perforation.

Deep creases of fear distorted his features. It was the kind of expression I'd woken up to in the bathroom mirror every day for the last ten years. The mortgage and my prostate and the coarse, grey hairs in my beard made me stare at myself in that same way. Curious, alarmed, stupid. Low print runs, shit sales, invasive editorial comments, the sneer of my wife, it all fucked my face up no differently than a couple of years of crank would have.

He wised up just a touch and decided to make a run for it. I angled myself in front of him. Church waddled over and sat behind me.

The prick said, "I'm a suicidal meth-head, bitch! I got nothing to lose!"

I cocked my chin and stared at him. He was in better shape than me and wore better clothing. I could see the bulge of a wallet in his front pocket. He might've stolen the cash but at least he had some. A gold chain with *Z Loves M* spelled out in diamonds hung from his neck. He had youth, gold, diamonds—he even had a girl.

Everything I owned was in the back seat of my car, packed into a couple of boxes and a rucksack. Church and I shared an old comforter for warmth. The pawn shop had everything else that my wife and the creditors hadn't taken. All the CDs, DVDs, first editions of my valuable books, my comic book collection, my signed posters, everything that had made me who I was would be making other men into who they were. My wallet didn't bulge. In it I had photos of my dead parents and my brother and me as kids, a driver's license with an invalid address, and a library card.

A voice that might've been mine said, "Well, come on then."

We circled each other and he made fitful hacking motions with the blade. I knew the correct way to defend myself was to take off my jacket and wrap it around my right arm. But there wasn't going to be any point to that. He was either going to get lucky and chop me through the sternum or I was going to break his wrist and stomp his guts. I already had both images firmly embedded in my mind.

I saw myself with the knife jutting from my chest, my eyes rolling back into my head, my legs giving out as I fell. There wouldn't be much blood. The knife would stop my heart almost instantly so there wouldn't be any arterial spray arcing out into traffic onto passing windshields. They'd drag me off and bury me in whatever landfill this city's potter's field passed for. They'd toss Churchill in the pound where he'd growl at all the little girls who made faces at him. They'd consider him unadoptable and give him a hotshot two weeks later.

I saw me reaching out with my left hand, my weak hand, yet somehow full of power at this moment, grabbing hold of his wrist and squeezing. The tiny bones grinding together and forcing a cry from his mouth. He'd hang onto the blade for a couple of seconds and then it would clatter to the cement. I'd tug him forward until we were nose to nose and I'd hiss, "Oh, Z, you just don't know what it means to have nothing to lose." It wouldn't be a good line. I wouldn't snap it off the way my protagonists might in my novels. It would hang in the air for too long and then I'd twist my hip into his groin and I'd duck and pull him forward across my back. He'd somersault in the air and land with a crunch. Vertebrae in his lower back would pop so loudly that Churchill would back away from the sound. Z would start wailing in pain. I knew how much lower back pain hurt. When I carried all the extra weight I'd get out of bed groaning and have to take a handful of pain medication and muscle relaxants to start my day. Then I'd kick Z in the forehead just hard enough to put him out.

I looked down and there he was, bleeding

from his scalp, unconscious but moaning like a lonely old man in his sleep. The mob around us began to move again.

I reached into his pocket and grabbed his bulging wallet. He was brazen enough to keep some packets of crystal stuffed in it. It seemed like no one else in the world held any fear of doing any fucking stupid or evil thing they felt like doing except for me. There was about eight hundred in cash. It would help keep me and Church going on the road to New York. I backed away and tossed his wallet on top of his chest. Then I turned and gathered up my things from the sidewalk.

I thought, Shit, I'm still not dead.

me wash my face in his bathroom and then packed my nost
e bridge of my nose. In a display of mercy he waved me forw
ose straight again. I swallowed a squeal while he placed his blu
tilage crackled and snapped. He let me wash my face in his ba
y nostrils with gauze and taped the bridge of my nose. In a
me forward and offered to set my nose straight again. I swal
ced his blunt hands on my face and cartilage crackled and s
 face in his bathroom and then packed my nostrils with gau
f my nose. In a display of mercy he waved me forward and
ight again. I swallowed a squeal while he placed his blunt ha
ge crackled and snapped. He let me wash my face in his ba
y nostrils with gauze and taped the bridge of my nose. In a
me forward and offered to set my nose straight again. I swal
ced his blunt hands on my face and cartilage crackled and s
 face in his bathroom and then packed my nostrils with gau
f my nose. In a display of mercy he waved me forward and
ight again. I swallowed a squeal while he placed his blunt ha
ge crackled and snapped. He let me wash my face in his ba
y nostrils with gauze and taped the bridge of my nose. In a
me forward and offered to set my nose straight again. I swal
ced his blunt hands on my face and cartilage crackled and s
 face in his bathroom and then packed my nostrils with gau
f my nose. In a display of mercy he waved me forward and
ight again. I swallowed a squeal while he placed his blunt ha
ge crackled and snapped. He let me wash my face in his ba
y nostrils with gauze and taped the bridge of my nose. In a
me forward and offered to set my nose straight again. I swal
ced his blunt hands on my face and cartilage crackled and s
 face in his bathroom and then packed my nostrils with gau
f my nose. In a display of mercy he waved me forward and
ight again. I swallowed a squeal while he placed his blunt ha
ge crackled and snapped. He let me wash my face in his ba
y nostrils with gauze and taped the bridge of my nose. In a
me forward and offered to set my nose straight again. I swal
ced his blunt hands on my face and cartilage crackled and s
 face in his bathroom and then packed my nostrils with ga
my nose. In a display of mercy he waved me forward and
ight again. I swallowed a squeal while he placed his blunt ha
ge used and snapped. He let me wash my face in his ba
nostrils with gauze and taped the bridge of my nose. In a

The guy in the nameless pawn shop took my father's coins and the battered remnants of my mother's prints from me. His shelves were stacked with the vestiges of my life. It was like walking into some alternate version of my house. Even a few literary awards I'd won over the years were tagged as paperweights and bookends.

In a display of mercy he waved me forward and offered to set my nose straight again. I swallowed a squeal while he placed his blunt hands on my face and cartilage crackled and snapped. He let me wash my face in his bathroom and then packed my nostrils with gauze and taped the bridge of my nose. When he was done he said, "Not so bad."

In the shine of his glass counter top I saw that my nose looked like hamburger. I glanced down at Church and he did a nervous little dance and snorted at my knee as if to push me back to the home we'd once had.

The pawn shop owner offered me a pittance for the coins and prints, the same as he'd robbed me on all the rest of my shit, but it was no less than I'd get anywhere else in these times. I took it.

Church groaned. He was hungry. We started for the door and were almost there when I turned.

The walk back to the counter was the longest walk I'd ever taken.

Longer than the stumbling blind flight from my mother's grave. Longer than the staggered half-jog from the bedroom following my wife as she carried her bags out to Sweetie's well-polished black truck. Longer than the shattering retreat down the driveway when

28

they hung the foreclosed sign on my front door.

Church began to whine. I looked down through the glass-top case. I pointed at one of the items.

The owner nodded.

"Good eye," he said.

I'd done a lot of research for a novel of mine entitled *The Bone Palace*. I'd printed out pages of material and studied up.

He unlocked the case and brought out the Smith & Wesson .38. I handed him back most of the money he'd just paid me. He set the .38 in my hand. I'd never held a gun before. I knew better than to dry fire it. I snapped it open, cocked the hammer, checked the line of sight. I eased the hammer back down. I'd done my homework.

He said, "I'll give you the cleaning equipment for free."

"Throw in a box of ammo too," I told him. "And a speed loader."

The voice still didn't sound like mine, but I

knew I was going to have to start recognizing it from now on.

His face registered some surprise. "Speed loaders are illegal."

"I know, but you've got them. I want one. Get it."

His lips parted and he started to argue, but I flared at him and he shut his mouth. He handed me some paperwork to fill out. I shoved it aside. He stared down at it and took a breath. I took one too. It went on like that for a dozen heartbeats or so. Then he got the ammo and the loader and slapped them on the counter in front of me. I filled my pockets. I caught sight of my reflection in the glass. My eyes were so black they looked like they'd been gouged out with an ice pick.

are too high. I am sacrificing myself and my blood on the
ocrity and the monthly terror of my mortgage. I am commit
ecause I'm too fat and lazy and intellectual to work a fact
e insurance. I am consigning my soul to hell because my ta
ficing myself and my blood on the ancient stone altar of me
rror of my mortgage. I am committing my baby to oblivion b
and intellectual to work a factory job where I can receive ins
soul to hell because my taxes are too high. I am sacrificing
he ancient stone altar of mediocrity and the monthly terro
mmitting my baby to oblivion because I'm too fat and la
a factory job where I can receive insurance. I am consign
e my taxes are too high. I am sacrificing myself and my bl
altar of mediocrity and the monthly terror of my mortgag
by to oblivion because I'm too fat and lazy and intellectual
e I can receive insurance. I am consigning my soul to hell b
gh. I am sacrificing myself and my blood on the ancient sto
the monthly terror of my mortgage. I am committing my
m too fat and lazy and intellectual to work a factory job
ce. I am consigning my soul to hell because my taxes are to
self and my blood on the ancient stone altar of mediocrity
ny mortgage. I am committing my baby to oblivion beca
d intellectual to work a factory job where I can receive insu
soul to hell because my taxes are too high. I am sacrificing
he ancient stone altar of mediocrity and the monthly terro
mmitting my baby to oblivion because I'm too fat and la

With the Rockies in my rearview I drove east across Denver and pulled into the drive-through of a fast food joint. I ordered four burgers and fries and a large drink. It's what I used to have for lunch every day when I was busy writing. No wonder I'd been so much fatter and softer and sleepy. No wonder my wife would have to climb up on top of me during sex because she didn't want my weight bearing down on her. No wonder the minimum wage kids would practically laugh in my face whenever they saw my fat ass pull up again.

I rolled down the driver's window and Churchill crawled over my lap and balanced himself against the driver's door with his chin jutting. When we got up to the cashier she was afraid to take my money. Church looked that hungry. I asked her for a cup of ice. She said it would cost an extra dollar.

"But I don't want another soda," I told her, "I just want some ice."

"It doesn't matter. That's what it costs."

"But it's just ice."

"That's what it costs."

My busted nose was throbbing badly. My eyes had started to get puffy and were just going to get worse until I couldn't drive. I had to get the swelling down.

"Do you have any aspirin in there?"

"Aspirin?"

"Yeah."

"We don't sell that."

"I know you don't sell that, I just wondered if you had any. For the employees maybe. In the first-aid kit."

"You're not an employee," she said. It wasn't snark, she was actually just reminding me.

"I'm aware of that."

"We don't have a first-aid kit. I have some in my purse, if you want them."

"Please, that would be great."

She vanished from the window for a moment and then returned. "I can't find them."

I smiled pleasantly at her. "Fine."

I smiled pleasantly at everyone. I smiled pleasantly at the bank guy who stuck the foreclosure sign on my front door. I smiled pleasantly when Church was a puppy and caught parvo and the vet told me to have him put down. I smiled pleasantly at my editor when the publisher remaindered two thousand copies of my last novel and I found them stacked in the thrift store with pink stickers, going for a quarter each, and still not selling.

After I picked up the food, I parked, fed Church three burgers, and ate the rest myself. He contentedly burped, passed gas, then circled the back seat and dug at the comforter until he laid down with a huff of air. He started to snore immediately.

I adjusted my seat back, wrapped the ice up in a couple of napkins, laid it on my face, and let myself drift to the music on an oldies station. I grew a little nostalgic while I hummed along. I sounded almost happy.

After an hour the ice had melted and the swelling had gone down. I got back on the road and floored it towards New York.

I'd come out to Colorado to be with my wife. We met on the Internet in a singles cafe. I really was that guy, she really was that girl. We met face to face in Vegas a few months later and started a long-distance relationship. I'd fly into Denver a couple of times a year and she'd come out to New York to visit me. She hated the bustle and action of Manhattan and spent most of her visits hiding in my apartment with the windows shut, tossing potpourri around to kill the smell of the city. Eventually came the point when one of us had to make a move or we'd have to split. I could do my job anywhere so I went to her.

The first few years were rough but righteous. I was slowly chipping out my career in the bedrock of publishing. I was the darling of the awards committees and won some pretty, shiny, tiny statues. I hoped the wins would translate into book sales. They didn't. The reviews got better but my advances got smaller. The bills stacked up. We were hurting financially but had reached a delayed yet progressive spiral of debt by borrowing from one credit company to pay the next, transferring the balance from the second card to pay down the first. I knew it would eventually lead us to hit the wall hard, but I hadn't expected the wall to rise up so soon or climb so high.

My wife refused to acknowledge the truth and continued buying whatever she wanted so long as it was on sale. Purchasing three pairs of shoes that had been marked down 30% was her way of helping out the situation. The fact that they'd originally cost $250 each didn't factor into the formula. Her math skills had always been weak.

I still held out hope though. I was as naive in my own way as she was in hers. I kept waiting for the break. The crossover. The big push. The major hit. You needed an insane amount of overconfidence to make it in the art world, but it usually cost you in other ways. I could fore-go health insurance because I saw myself one day teaching at an Ivy League school and passing on my fount of knowledge. I didn't need a European vacation because we'd eventually own a villa on the coast of France like every other hotshot bestseller. Whatever was missing today would be made up for later. I held onto the chance like a retarded kid unwilling to give up a broken toy.

The grey in my beard didn't wake me up to reality, but the grey pubes started to spook me a touch.

Then she got pregnant. My unsophisticated

dreams managed to press back the edges of a clinical depression. Church sensed the difference and started prancing around the house like a happy uncle ready to pass out cigars in the waiting room.

The word father took on a whole new meaning. It stopped being about my old man and started being about me. I saw a little girl in a pink bed holding her arms up and calling for "Daddy" after a bad dream. I saw myself sitting in my library recliner with the kid on my lap, reading her *Through the Looking Glass*.

My wife wasn't as certain about being a mother, but she was willing to ride it out until the serious pain hit and she began to spot. The doctor told her to stay in bed for the next twelve weeks. My wife liked to go out dancing, if not with me than with her friends. Some of the friends were male. I wasn't jealous, or at least not as jealous as I should've been. I stewed behind my obesity and ate even more. I sometimes stopped off at the ice cream shop across the street from the club where she liked to go on Friday nights. Churchill was especially fond of butter pecan.

She talked abortion. I stayed up night after night sweating it out. I wanted kids. I didn't want to be alone with my wife for the rest of my life. I knew we were falling apart even then. I didn't just want glue to hold us together. I wanted someone who needed me, who would help me to fulfill the myth of myself. I thought I could wake up to cries in the middle of the night almost happily. I would pick up my little girl and shush her with my lips to her chubby cheek and press my forehead to hers and will all my love into her life. She would quiet and coo and giggle, and I'd put her back on her pink pillows and stare at her for another hour in the dim grey light of the wolf's hour.

But my anxiety medication didn't always help out. My mind raced and my teeth buzzed. The money wasn't there. The marriage was on the skids. I'd overshot being a father by years. I was old and fat. I needed silence when I wrote. I wasn't going to suddenly get strong and pure this late in life. I was greedy. I didn't want upset, I'd already had enough of that. How was I going to have a kid when I had no benefits? How was I going to pay off the hospital, the babysitters, the pre-K, the clothes, the food, the college tuition? I heard the baby screeching and wailing and it wouldn't stop and I was too lazy to get out of bed on my darkest days when the antidepressants weren't working.

She made an appointment. That morning, I followed along after her in a state of trauma. I felt the same way I had while watching my mother's heart monitor continuously slow throughout the course of her last night, stalling, redlining as her breaths came in agonized gasps, and I found myself halfway between hoping it would end and wanting to scream out, "Mommy." I trotted after my wife to the car and drove to Planned Parenthood.

Protesters walked their picket line in the freezing morning air, calling for me not to murder my own child, saying my baby wanted to live, please give it a chance at life.

Christ, if only I'd had a gun on me then. I would have killed every one of those fuckers. I would have used the speed loader until my flesh seared and the shells were too hot to handle. The cops would have potshot and tasered and billy clubbed me before dragging me away in cuffs while I shrieked. I wouldn't have been able to stand trial. They would have put me in a rubber room. I would have butted my head against the soft walls in a straitjacket, rocking like a newborn myself. Christ fuckall, if only.

I sat in the waiting room with young men who looked expectantly relieved. Some of them were boyfriends, some only one-night stands. Some might've been husbands who, like me, thought about bills instead of baby booties.

At that moment I realized, This is the thing I will never be forgiven for. This is what is now being written in the great Book of Life by the weeping saints and martyrs. This is the moment God will point to with his burning hand at the hour of my death. This is my chance to have and love my own child and I am freely passing it by. I am committing my baby to oblivion because I'm too fat and lazy and intellectual to work a factory job where I can receive insurance. I am consigning my soul to hell because my taxes are too high. I am sacrificing myself and my blood on the ancient stone altar of mediocrity and the monthly terror of my mortgage.

A nurse appeared and told me it was all over. And it was.

Maybe he ought to stay up there on the cross and keep doing his own thing. Maybe God should stay out of the Sunday literary supplements. Maybe he ought to stay up there on the cross and keep doing his own thing. Maybe God should stay out of the Sunday literary supplements. Maybe he ought to stay up there on the cross and keep doing his own thing. Maybe God should stay out of the Sunday literary supplements. Maybe he ought to stay up there on the cross and keep doing his own thing. Maybe God should stay out of the Sunday literary supplements. Maybe he ought to stay up there on the cross and keep doing his own thing. Maybe God should stay out of the Sunday literary supplements. Maybe he ought to stay up there on the cross and keep doing his own thing. Maybe God should stay out of the Sunday literary supplements. Maybe he ought to stay up there on the cross and keep doing his own thing. Maybe God should stay out of the Sunday literary supplements.

I hadn't mapped out my return home. I didn't want to shoot back in a straight line. I wanted to do whatever I could to forestall the next step along my journey of the inevitable. I crossed into Kansas and saw flat empty farmland from the flat empty highway. I spotted an exit that promised gas and food and wound up driving through a dead town that looked like the plague had hit it.

I got back on the highway and passed two other exits before getting off and finding the same thing. Main Street was lined by barren stores with For Rent signs in the windows. Abandoned houses on the outskirts had foreclosure signs slapped on the doors. The word itself made me tighten my fists on the steering wheel. Church glanced up at me nervously. I wheeled past collapsed barns and stone wall-bordered weed-choked fields.

We were looking at the days of the dust bowl gangsters again. When your average citizen was losing everything, they were forced into desperate, mad actions. Bank robbery attempts were at a thirty-year high. A husband and wife team had tried to take down my local bank and been wiped out by six cops in the parking lot, a couple thousand bucks in hand.

The media replayed the surveillance footage for weeks. Just before they'd been cut down the couple wore expressions that said they wanted to take the whole thing back if only anyone would grant them a do-over. My old man wore the same expression on his deathbed. I looked in the rearview and thought I was getting there fast.

I did what I usually did. I wrote in my head. The words drifted in and out, the music of the language singing in my ear. I edited as I went. I had visions of what should be happening. There ought to be a hot teenage girl hitchhiking along the side of the road. She would bring me wild pain and nights of burning glory and ultimate redemption.

She would mark me with her teeth and I would battle the demons from her past. Maybe a dirty cop who was hounding her just to squeeze information out of her about her drug lord ex-boyfriend. I'd have to be smarter than everybody, sharp enough to take care of the cop, the boyfriend's killer thugs, the boyfriend who raised piranha, kept a stable of whores, and who'd act friendly to me at first before pulling out a straight razor. He'd slash open one side of my face and maybe take an eye, but I'd overcome because I was pure of soul. The hitchhiking honey with the breeze in her hair and the gams that didn't quit would love my scarred and brutalized face anyway.

I didn't have much but I still had the urge to write. The stories went on and on. I wondered if that would ultimately save me or only doom me further. Was I finally going to write my masterpiece or just hack out an angry vapid potboiler because friends of mine had made money writing angry vapid potboilers?

I checked off the topics and narrative elements that were hot in publishing right now. Vampire tween romances: When you got down to it that was pretty fucking creepy, really. Centuries-old teenage vampire males sexing up sixteen-year-old sophomore human chippie gals. Then there were the Christian metaphors couched in heart-tugger tales about women having to raise the spoiled children of their condemned sisters about to get the chair on death row. What else, what else. Zombie mashups with classics of literature. Nobody took them seriously, not even the millions of people who bought them.

The hit authors showed up on daytime talk shows explaining how their characters had whispered in their ears and the books had written themselves. One bestseller called it a divine cathartic expulsion. She claimed God had moved through her body and into her fingers and had tapped out her novel about a werewolf waitress who falls in love with the sous-chef. Her next book was about an alien who comes to earth to coach a pee-wee football league and gives up his homeworld to court a divorcee with a chip on her shoulder. The audience went wild. The host had tears in her eyes.

Maybe God should stay out of the Sunday literary supplements. Maybe he ought to stay up there on the cross and keep doing his own thing.

I didn't have a laptop anymore but I'd brought along a bunch of legal pads and pencils. In truck stops I drank coffee for hours while I filled page after page with a furious angular script I had trouble reading. I slept at the rest stops with Churchill on top of my chest. I sometimes woke up with Church shivering, and I knew I'd been talking or crying in my sleep. He picked up on my mood and shook and groaned. It sometimes took me half an hour to get him calm again.

I'd get behind the wheel once more and drive the black roads leading me back into the shadows of my own past. It wasn't going to get me anywhere. I knew it was going to all be another big mistake in a lifetime of gaffes.

I drove with one hand in my pocket. I'd fondle the unloaded gun and think about going on a rampage of some sort. But I couldn't figure out what kind. Who would I take hostage, what would my demands be? How much money would be enough? Where would I want them to fly the jet? Which of the quirky bank patrons and employees was I going to let go first? The elderly old man with the heart trouble or the pregnant Korean lady? What kind of food would I ask for while the negotiations were going on? I hadn't had New York pizza in ten years. I imagined the SWAT guy pretending to be a pizza delivery kid, a stack of pepperoni pies in his arms, the top box empty except for a semi-automatic.

He'd dump the boxes and point the weapon and scream for me to put my hands up.

And all I would be able to do was look at the wasted pepperoni pies on the floor, my mouth watering.

assing up salvation. Maybe I needed to pull over and find s
s I was. The girl wouldn't know the truth. She'd be a sloppy
assing up salvation. Maybe I needed to pull over and find s
s I was. The girl wouldn't know the truth. She'd be a sloppy
assing up salvation. Maybe I needed to pull over and find s
s I was. The girl wouldn't know the truth. She'd be a sloppy
assing up salvation. Maybe I needed to pull over and find s
s I was. The girl wouldn't know the truth. She'd be a sloppy
assing up salvation. Maybe I needed to pull over and find s
s I was. The girl wouldn't know the truth. She'd be a sloppy
assing up salvation. Maybe I needed to pull over and find s
s I was. The girl wouldn't know the truth. She'd be a sloppy
assing up salvation. Maybe I needed to pull over and find s
s I was. The girl wouldn't know the truth. She'd be a sloppy
assing up salvation. Maybe I needed to pull over and find s
s I was. The girl wouldn't know the truth. She'd be a sloppy
assing up salvation. Maybe I needed to pull over and find s
s I was. The girl wouldn't know the truth. She'd be a sloppy
assing up salvation. Maybe I needed to pull over and find s
s I was. The girl wouldn't know the truth. She'd be a sloppy
assing up salvation. Maybe I needed to pull over and find s

T he thunderstorms started to hit in Missouri but I bulled my way through hour after hour while the rain smashed down. Even with my wipers on extra high they could barely keep up with the torrent. Visibility was practically nil. Flares lined the highways where fatal pileups had occurred. The state patrol beckoned and diverted traffic through the hills and hollers of Appalachia. Cinder block houses and hammered tin roof trailers dotted the grubby landscape. They still let their kids play barefoot in the flooded meadows and thickets. Every fourth shotgun shack for a hundred muddy miles had an underage girl-with long wet hair and a bare midriff on the porch, waving a highball glass at me.

Maybe I was passing up salvation. Maybe I needed to pull over and find someone nearly as bad off as I was. The girl wouldn't know the truth. She'd be a sloppy but fun lay. We'd get wasted on moonshine with too much radiator fluid in it. She'd be secretly pleased with my Yankee accent. She'd think I was the one who would get her out of this town and take her someplace else where she could shine in the bright lights, be a model or actress on Broadway. Her father would chase me with a ten-gauge and I wouldn't run all that fast to get away from him. They shot horses, put rabid dogs down, drowned starving cats, butchered hogs. This might be the place to get done right.

On the wrong side of a washed-out bridge somewhere in southern Illinois I was forced to hole up in a place called the Sweet Pea Motel. Church and I laid together on the double bed and watched cable and ate from the candy machine. There was a diner next door that charged extra for delivery in the storm. We had fried chicken and BLTs and fresh apple pie. The delivery kid was drenched head to foot but looked happy to be getting the extra buck per order.

The storm continued but Church and I didn't mind. We were living better than we had in weeks. Z's cash came in handy. I was stupid not to have cleaned out the pockets of the two other punks.

Having maid service was like being taken care of by a loved one. I took hour-long hot showers. I ordered pay-per-view movies. I'd forgotten how much I liked to sit back and just watch a flick. Church did his business six inches outside the motel door and the swirling rainwater immediately cleared it away.

I scrawled on the legal pads. I didn't even know what I was writing. Maybe it was a novel, maybe a journal. Maybe it was a manifesto. Or a love letter. Or a suicide note or my last will and testament. The pages filled up and I didn't reread them. When the writing was good it felt like bleeding onto the page. That's how I felt now. I slept deeply without dreams.

The emergency newsbreaks told of mass flooding. Rivers overflowing, whole towns being washed away. I walked over to the diner through a swirling two-foot-deep vortex in the parking lot, holding Churchill in my arms. The waitress and the cook were husband and wife and lived in back of the place. They had the same worried look stamped into their faces every time I saw them. They were in danger of losing their business, their home, their livelihood.

The delivery truck couldn't make it through one morning and provisions started running low. But they still managed to have fresh pie. I ate happily. So did Church. The waitress sat with us and stared out the window with terror in her eyes. She patted Church's back until he went to sleep in the booth beside her. His snores were loud but not loud enough to cover the sound of the relentless, endless rain.

Back at the Sweet Pea Motel I kept writing.

I think I went on for a few pages about the drowning world, but I couldn't be sure. I watched more movies. I sat glued to the news and saw volunteer workers filling sandbags at the edges of various murderous rivers. Three states were declared disaster areas and the National Guard was sent out to aid the citizens.

On the fifth day the ceiling bloated and began to leak through. The manager brought me more ice buckets and waste pails. I spread them around the room under the worst of the drips and the hard ticking and ringing was like being surrounded by a dozen clocks counting off the wasted hours.

I began toying with the gun. I loaded it and unloaded it. I fit ammo into the speed loader so I could snap all six bullets in at once. I kept writing.

The storm became metaphor. It was literary technique: As below, so above. When the hero suffered, so did the rest of the world. My hand cramped up and I sat on the edge of the bed massaging my fingers. My knuckles cracked as if someone was taking a hammer to them.

I wondered if the methers in front of the pawn shop were in my book. I wondered what I was saying about my wife. I could imagine my mother's values and my father's lessons filling paragraph after paragraph. Would the story end with a tidal wave washing away the Sweet Pea? I thought Church standing on the roof riding it like a surfboard would make for a hell of a cover. Novels with covers that had dogs on them almost always sold a ton of copies.

On the seventh day the rain stopped and the sky started to clear. The waters slowly began to recede. The news showed the president helping to pump water out of a homeless shelter's basement.

The diner was completely out of food by then. I was living on the vending machine snacks. It took another three days before the highway reopened. The delivery truck came through. I got to have a last BLT and slice of pie. I settled my bill at the motel. My car started on the first try.

I rolled the windows down and Churchill hung his head out and caught some sun. We hit the road heading east. When we were between towns, without another car in sight, I pulled the .38 and held it out the driver's window straight up in the air and fired it like a starter's pistol. The recoil wasn't nearly as bad as I'd been expecting. No man should ever have a gun without firing it at least once, just to know what it felt like.

Now I knew.

New York, I'm coming home.

it all you have to do is come home to find out how. You rea
e wrong side of the expressway for miles and miles until sr
ghtliner. Everybody's always stunned that it could have hap
do is come home to find out how. You read about assholes
the expressway for miles and miles until smacking head-
ybody's always stunned that it could have happened, but
e home to find out how. You read about assholes driving th
way for miles and miles until smacking head-on into a frei
s stunned that it could have happened, but all you have
d out how. You read about assholes driving the wrong sid
es and miles until smacking head-on into a freightliner. Ever
at it could have happened, but all you have to do is come
read about assholes driving the wrong side of the express
til smacking head-on into a freightliner. Everybody's always
happened, but all you have to do is come home to find o
sholes driving the wrong side of the expressway for miles ar
d-on into a freightliner. Everybody's always stunned that
it all you have to do is come home to find out how. You rea
e wrong side of the expressway for miles and miles until sr
ghtliner. Everybody's always stunned that it could have hap
do is come home to find out how. You read about assholes
the expressway for miles and miles until smacking head-
ybody's always stunned that it could have happened, but
e home to find out how. You read about assholes driving th
way for miles and miles until smacking head-on into a frei
s stunned that it could have happened, but all you have
d out how. You read about assholes driving the wrong sid

At around midnight I parked in front of my brother's house on Long Island and watched him through his huge bay window. He was ten years older than me and looked at least five years younger. He'd never had to watch his weight. I had more grey in my hair. He refused to go for glasses. He held the newspaper at arm's length and squinted and pretended he was still nineteen years old. He turned out the lamp and went up to his bedroom, and after an hour he shut out the light and the house went dark. I got out and took a piss on his neighbor's lawn and Church took a shit. We got back in the car.

My brother's prostate must've been bothering him. He got up several times during the night. At least once he came down to the kitchen. I caught a glimpse of him at the refrigerator. In the pale yellow glow he appeared dissatisfied and restless. He made himself half a cucumber sandwich. My brother was big on half-portions. He'd eat half an orange, drink half a bottle of water, chop a tomato perfectly in half for a salad and then wrap up the remainder carefully in plastic.

My thoughts kept flitting. I wondered how many photos of us he had in his house. I wondered why he hadn't found the time to visit the old man or Ma right before the end. I wondered why I'd called him after my marriage went bust. It was the last thing I should have done.

I crawled into the back seat and got under the blanket and did my best to get comfortable in the cramped space. I wasn't ready to face him yet. Maybe I never would be. This might be the worst misstep yet.

Church climbed on top of me and stretched

out on my stomach. He missed my fat belly. For him it had been like a waterbed.

My brother had appeared in a lot of my fiction under a variety of guises. He was the villainous father figure in at least two of my novels. He was sometimes the best friend whose expression of disappointment eventually leads my protagonist to betray him. I'd written about the love I'd felt for him when I was a boy and he'd ride his ten-speed around our hometown with me on the handlebars, coasting into the corner stationary and buying me comics. Presenting me to his girlfriends and telling them how smart and talented I was. I used to show him my early stories and he would critique without criticizing. He would encourage and compliment. He would write inspiring notes across the top of the loose leaf pages: You're going to go all the way, kid!

I slept a few hours and then got up and turned the dome light on. I pulled out my wallet and looked at the picture of us when we were kids. I was seven, he was seventeen.

We're both grinning like crazy. We're at the beach. He's muscular with a resigned air of power and hepcat cool. I'm cheesing it up with my front teeth missing. He looks like our father. I don't look like anybody.

Our falling out was still a few years off. When I became a teenager his affection for me faltered. He grew hypercritical. He became domineering, overbearing, teasing and downright nasty. He seethed and hissed at me. I wasn't athletic. I couldn't catch a football. I didn't lift weights. When we played basketball in the driveway he was always eager to throw an elbow into my bulging gut. He talked about making me stronger and healthier. He acted like an angry, frustrated parent. I brought home straight *As* but they weren't straight enough. I was too slovenly, I was already gaining weight. I didn't get outside enough, I read too much, I watched too much TV, I wasted money on kid stuff like comic books. He got his own apartment and I'd ride my bike over there and knock on the door. I'd see the blinds flutter but he wouldn't answer.

I still didn't know why it had gone so wrong. Maybe he had his own premonitions and visions too. Maybe he saw what lay ahead of me and hated me for it. Or himself. Maybe he'd been warning me all along, and I just hadn't listened.

We'd seen each other at weddings and funerals but he'd never visited me out west and I'd never been to his house on the island, even though he lived in the same town where we'd grown up.

The sky began to lighten to a purple blur. I pulled away from the curb and drove through town with my hackles up. It looked familiar but didn't feel that way. I had that same nervous feeling you got whenever you were lost in some unfamiliar city. Everything put the shits up you. You looked at the faces on the street and wondered which one of them might make a sudden dash for your car and smash the windshield with a brick. You wondered if you might be reading the street signs wrong or heading down a one-way going in the wrong direction. You read about assholes driving the wrong side of the expressway for miles and miles until smacking head-on into a freightliner. Everybody's always stunned that it could have happened, but all you have to do is come home to find out how. It's the same feeling. That you're doing something wrong but you can't put your finger on it.

The sun climbed. I passed my parents' house. What used to be my parents' house. My brother and I had sold it after our mother died. I spotted a few moderate changes here and there but was surprised it still looked practically the same after all this time. I could imagine my father sitting on the stoop watering the lawn. I could see my mother trimming her roses, wearing men's working gloves, a kerchief tying her hair up. A smear of mud across her forehead from where she'd wiped sweat away with the back of her hand. My old man occasionally swinging the nozzle of the hose and flicking water at her. Ma shrieking like a little girl, Dad laughing loudly.

My brother in the driveway, his head under the hood of a car. Three drops of oil splashed on his tight T-shirt. Thick black veins twisting up his powerful forearms. Every so often a car full of girls would drive by and stop at the curb. They'd wave and call to him and he'd trot down to the street and lean in the window and smile, cool as could be, hip, virile, in charge, and the girls giggling, and he'd pinch one of their chins between thumb and forefinger and leave a dash of oil on her face. They'd drive off to some party and he'd finish up on the car, slam the hood shut, wash his hands with pumice stone, put on a fresh T-shirt, and then follow after.

I was there in front of the house long enough for an angry face to appear at the front door. I remembered the guy from the closing. He'd been freshly married then. He and his wife were ecstatic about buying their first home. I left a bottle of wine on the counter along with the extra sets of keys.

Now he looked like he was ready to defend the place with his life. If anyone dared to step foot on his property he'd grab up a shotgun. His eyes burned like twin lakes of flaming gasoline. He'd hold the bankers at bay, the police, the SWAT teams, the communists, the alien hordes, the barbaric populace of disintegrating cities. I thought I should've done it myself. I should have mined the yard. I should have held out at the front window with a rifle in my hands. I should have protected my home. I should have fought for it. I should have died for it.

I gave the guy a little salute.

He glowered and rushed out and started to run at my car. I didn't know what troubles he had on his mind but there must've been plenty of them. Maybe he thought I was a bill collector or a process server. Maybe his wife had left him and was sending her lawyer around. Or maybe he recognized me after all and wanted me to take back the house and everything that went along with it. Busted water pipes, termites, damp rot. County taxes, hazard insurance, backed up cesspool. I stomped the gas pedal and ripped out down the street. He fell in behind me and sprinted a hundred yards before he finally took a tumble and lay on the asphalt sucking wind. I almost went back to lend him a hand. Or to drive over his throat.

ach other crazy. This is how it usually went. We confused ea
ch other. We looked enough alike to remind each other of o
ap warped glass. We drove each other crazy. This is how
ed each other. We distrusted each other. We looked eno
ther of ourselves seen through cheap warped glass. We dr
is how it usually went. We confused each other. We distrus
enough alike to remind each other of ourselves seen throu
e drove each other crazy. This is how it usually went. We
istrusted each other. We looked enough alike to remind ea
through cheap warped glass. We drove each other craz
nt. We confused each other. We distrusted each other. W
emind each other of ourselves seen through cheap warp
ther crazy. This is how it usually went. We confused each o
ther. We looked enough alike to remind each other of ourse
arped glass. We drove each other crazy. This is how it usua
h other. We distrusted each other. We looked enough alike t
selves seen through cheap warped glass. We drove each oth
ually went. We confused each other. We distrusted each o
like to remind each other of ourselves seen through cheap
ach other crazy. This is how it usually went. We confused ea
ch other. We looked enough alike to remind each other of o
ap warped glass. We drove each other crazy. This is how
ed each other. We distrusted each other. We looked eno
ther of ourselves seen through cheap warped glass. We d
is how it usually went. We confused each other. We distru
enough alike to remind each other of ourselves seen

I killed most of the day. I don't know how. I circled town going nowhere, looking at nothing for hours. We had lunch at another fast food place. Church enjoyed his burgers. I knew I wasn't doing him any favours by feeding him that shit, but he loved it. He slept and I circled some more, drove down to the bay, then north to the sound, then out east to the lighthouse. We walked along the beach for a while. I think I wrote some more.

Finally I pulled into my brother's driveway. It was time to face him. He heard my car door slam and moved to stand at his bay window. As I crossed the yard he nodded to me without expression, but he still managed that chuckle of self-righteousness. I smiled pleasantly. I hadn't showered or changed my clothes in four days. At his front door he sniffed and brought the back of his hand to cover his nose, but to his credit he didn't say anything about it.

He gave me the first of the sad, slow once-overs. I knew more would be coming.

"You've lost weight," he said.

"Yes, I have," I agreed.

"A lot of it."

"Yeah."

The next thing to say would naturally be that I looked good. Except he didn't because I didn't.

He turned his head and glanced at me askew. "Your nose."

"My nose?"

"What's different about your nose?"

I knew what he meant. "What do you mean?"

"It's . . . bent. A little crooked."

"You need glasses, man."

He did but he'd never admit it, just like I'd never admit that my nose was a little more spread out across my face. He turned away and nodded to himself, agreeing with who knows what the fuck kind of misgivings and suspicions he already had. "You've been fighting."

"Not too much," I said.

Church yawned loudly enough to get noticed. My brother looked down at him and pulled a face. "You have a dog."

"His name is Churchill."

"An English bulldog named after the most famous English Prime Minister. Cute."

He didn't think it was cute. My brother hated dogs. Church yawned again. I was starting to sweat and feel a little wobbly on my legs. It had been a long ride and it still wasn't over. Seeing my brother only proved that I wasn't home, that I had no home to go to ever again.

"You look feverish," he said.

"I got caught in the flood."

"The flood?" He flicked his tongue like the word tasted bad to him. "Which flood?"

"Any flood. All floods are the same."

"They're the same?"

"There's lots of water."

"What are you talking about?" he asked.

"What are *you* talking about?" I countered.

This is how it usually went. We confused each other. We distrusted each other. We looked enough alike to remind each other of ourselves seen through cheap warped glass. We drove each other crazy.

I was still on his front porch. We both noticed at the same time and he backed out of the doorway and said, "Come on in."

"Thanks."

"The dog is house-trained?"

"Yes, Churchill is."

My brother's expression shifted again. It showed doubt and dismay and apprehension. He had a thousand of these faces he could pull. Ten thousand. I knew I'd see a lot more of them before the night was out. "Okay then."

I stepped in and Churchill followed and my brother walked us down the main hall directly into the kitchen like he was ushering caterers to set up for a party. The whole place sparkled so brightly it took my eyes a few seconds to get used to it. Copper pots and pans hung from the ceiling over the centre island. The stink of lemon-scented cleaners made my mouth pucker. He'd grown even more fastidious in his old age.

"Are you hungry?" he asked.

"Yes."

"I was about to make myself a steak. Want one?"

"Sure."

He opened the fridge and stared at the beer for a while before making up his mind that alcohol wasn't a part of my problem. Then he offered me one. I took it, sipped, and sat.

I knew he was going to only make himself

half a steak. I wondered if he was going to offer me just the other half or actually make a separate T-bone for me. He wavered, thinking about it himself, and then drew out two slabs of thawing meat from the lowest shelf. Churchill perked up and wandered over to my brother, his stubby tail wagging, his hindquarters swaying. He let out a growl of joy.

I watched my brother carefully as he broiled the steaks, chopped vegetables, made a fruit cocktail, and threw dashes of spices across the various plates and bowls. He moved around the kitchen in ways that reminded me of both my mother and my father. There was a muscular, powerful presence to him and also a delicate agility. Once he bent too sharply and his knees cracked as loudly as rifle shots.

We made small talk. It was so small that we couldn't even find it moment to moment. Our voices trailed off. The hum of the microwave made us repeat things that didn't even matter the first time around. He told me about his job. I told him about the flood. He told me about some kind of weed killer he found very effective. I told him that Churchill was up to date on his shots. He told me it was going to be sunny for the next few days. I told him about my latest nomination for a literary award.

He asked me if there was any money involved.

I asked him, Well, what the fuck do you think?

I enjoyed the salad and had another beer. He fixed us both plates with lots of garnishes and fed me well. The T-bone was perfect, and I ate quickly. I hadn't realized I'd been so hungry. Right before I finished up he cut his own steak in half and put the extra piece on my plate. It was an oddly affectionate gesture, the kind my father would have made.

Churchill kept waiting for me to toss the bone on the floor for him, but there was no need to provoke my brother. He was having a hard enough time already. I put Church out in the yard and threw the bone to him. It would keep him busy for hours. Even before he got his teeth on it he barked at it and cavorted wildly. Then he threw his cannonball bulk at it and started to chew.

I sat again and sipped my beer. My brother laid his knife and fork across the centre of his plate, sat back in his seat, and eyed me.

"She was never right for you," he said.

"You're probably right," I admitted.

And there it was. In three seconds of conversation we'd pretty much wiped out the last decade of my life. I wondered what other slates we were about to clear.

The conversation danced around. I drank more beer but felt as sober as I'd ever felt in my life. Every so often one of us would ask a real question or make a bold statement. The other would mostly divert and dive for cover. He brought out a devil's food cake and ate half a piece.

I couldn't figure out why he didn't have a woman. When he was twenty-one, with biceps the size of cannonballs, he always had a girl around. They never lasted long but I always figured that was because he was playing the field. Maybe I'd been wrong. For all I knew he was gay or asexual. I should've had the nerve, curiosity, or the concern to ask, but I just didn't.

"Have you been to the cemetery lately?" I asked.

His lips smoothed into a bloodless line. "Every week."

"Why so often?"

He shrugged his broad shoulders. I thought with shoulders like that I'd be able to rule the world. "It relaxes me. I go out there and walk the little paths through the place. Bring a few flowers, say some prayers. The ritual of it helps me to meditate."

"I didn't know you meditated."

"I don't except when I'm there."

Exhaustion hit me heavily. I glanced at the window and saw it was dark outside. I'd lost another day to the haze. I went to the back door and called Church. He pranced inside, his muzzle covered with marrow. I sat again and

Church flopped at my feet and immediately went to sleep. His snores soon began to rattle the copper pots.

My brother kept scrutinizing Church. He was already worried about the dog. His eyes flashed with visions of shit-stained carpets, pee-soaked couch cushions, shredded throw pillows, having his throat torn out in his sleep. His breathing grew more rapid. I wondered if he was going to suddenly grab up a frying pan and attack my sleeping dog. I glanced around for a weapon. I spotted a ladle. In a clutch it might still prove useful. I imagined my brother and I in a death match involving kitchen utensils. I saw us wrestling and bleeding across his immensely clean floor, me whacking him over the head trying to crush his skull with the ladle. I could hear the ka-bong of the frying pan smashing my jaw, could almost feel my teeth rattling loose in my head. I don't know why I didn't see myself drawing the gun. I seemed to keep forgetting there was a gun.

"You're always welcome here," he said, "but the dog stays in the garage. He stinks."

I heard the hanging implication in his voice. He meant, The dog stinks even worse than you.

"I'll give him a bath," I said.

"That's not good enough. Then the house will just smell like wet dog, and that's even worse."

"I'll dry him."

"Don't argue, right?" he said.

I looked deep into my brother's face. As usual, there was no give there, no mercy. He always held his chin high, his shoulders squared. It was a good tactic that made him more imposing. He was still tall and muscular and cut a real swath. His eyes were hard as shale.

I got up, shook his hand and said, "Good seeing you," then started for the door. "Thanks for dinner." Churchill grumbled as he climbed to his feet and followed me.

"You're leaving?" my brother asked.

"Yes."

"Because of a dog?"

There was no way to explain it to him so I just said, "Yes, because of a dog."

"What the hell has happened to you?"

"Is that the question you're really asking?"

He gave me the sad long once-over and shook his head sorrowfully. He couldn't meet my gaze. "All right, the dog can stay in the house. But give him a fucking bath now. And he doesn't roam the house until he's completely dry. And if he pisses or shits inside even once, he's in the garage for good."

That sounded fair. And all I was looking for was fair.

labor and my life? Did he want me to ask myself, Was it w
my accomplishments are. A child could carry them all away
left my books here because he knew that one day I'd lose ev
ome stay with him? So I could see, packed into thirty inches
of my labor and my life? Did he want me to ask myself, Was
all my accomplishments are. A child could carry them all a
ad he left my books here because he knew that one day
forced to come stay with him? So I could see, packed in
ace, all the fruits of my labor and my life? Did he want m
th it? Look at how small my accomplishments are. A chi
y in a tiny red wagon. Had he left my books here because
se everything and be forced to come stay with him? So I co
inches of shelf space, all the fruits of my labor and my life
self, Was it worth it? Look at how small my accomplishmen
nem all away in a tiny red wagon. Had he left my books here
day I'd lose everything and be forced to come stay with h
into thirty inches of shelf space, all the fruits of my labor
to ask myself, Was it worth it? Look at how small my accompli
carry them all away in a tiny red wagon. Had he left my boo
that one day I'd lose everything and be forced to come s
e, packed into thirty inches of shelf space, all the fruits of
he want me to ask myself, Was it worth it? Look at how s
are. A child could carry them all away in a tiny red wagon
because he knew that one day I'd lose everything and be
So I could see, packed into thirty inches
d my life? Did he want

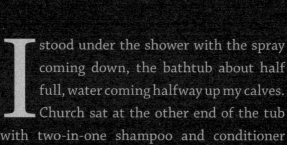

I stood under the shower with the spray coming down, the bathtub about half full, water coming halfway up my calves. Church sat at the other end of the tub with two-in-one shampoo and conditioner worked into his fur and a pile of bubbles on top of his head. He didn't look amused. My brother wasn't going to be either.

I still thought it would make a funny scene in the movie version of my memoirs, with some B-grade beefcake actor playing the loose cannon dude in the shower with the trained dog barking on command. There would be witty dialogue because I wouldn't be the screenwriter. The guy would say something cute to the dog, and the dog would make funny faces and groan and belch, and the audience would laugh. On the daytime talk shows the screenwriter could say he wrote the script in a divine cathartic expulsion. God moved through his body and into his fingers. The host would have tears in her eyes.

I got out and towelled off. Then I drained the tub and rinsed Churchill and dried him too. My brother had a lot of aftershave, colognes, and body powders on his bathroom counter. Too many, I thought, but who was I to judge.

My brother was sitting in his den with his feet up on an ottoman, reading a celebrity magazine. It surprised me more than anything else we'd talked about all day. I'd never have imagined him reading that kind of thing. Then again, he was squinting so badly that maybe he thought he was reading the *Wall Street Journal*.

He looked up and said, "You're tired. Go get some sleep."

"Okay, thanks."

I turned to go and he said, "So what are your plans?"

"To go to bed."

"After that."

My shoulders tensed and my stomach tightened. "Dream the dreams of the righteous."

It made him toss his magazine aside. He couldn't quite hit me with his usual glare, but a dark light filled his eyes. There was sadness in there, and even some humility, but still no mercy. My brother liked to educate and advise and nail down matters of large import, especially if they weren't his own.

I cocked my head at him and wondered which topic he was going to tackle right now. What he was going to tell me to do first thing in the morning? Shave my beard? Find a job? Hit the gym? Check in with the collection agencies and start the long process of cleaning up my credit score? Meditate at the cemetery? I waited expectantly. He wet his lips. He stared at my dog. He sniffed the air and could only smell his own body powder. Church had a dab of it on his ass still.

But the light in his eyes dimmed and he sat back in his chair. He reached for the magazine again. He nodded to himself once more. I wish I could hear the conversations he had with himself in his head. His inner voice seemed to always be agreeing with him, he was always nodding along. Yeah, yeah, yeah.

He turned back to me and said, "See you in the morning."

"Right."

The guest room was larger than the master bedroom in my former house. It was freshly painted in sky blue and decorated in a country style, with lots of natural wood and wicker. I was thankful there wasn't a butter churn or wagon wheel in the corner. I'd been right about the fruity air freshener. It spritzed the air on a timer and made the place smell like a funeral parlour.

Folded up neatly at the foot of the bed was a blanket my mother had nearly finished crocheting during her final days in the hospital, waiting for the docs to fix her varicose veins. I was surprised and glad to see it again.

On a perfectly dusted shelf smelling of pine oil stood all of my novels. I'd sent him a copy of each one of my books through some irrepressible sense of pride. The spines had never been cracked. I hadn't expected them to be. But shit, to discover that he chose the celebrity weekly gossip mags over me, that hurt a bit.

I wondered why he kept my novels in the guest room. Was it merely as decoration? The books, taken as a whole, had nice colourful covers. Or was he actually offering them up as entertainment to his guests, whoever and however many of them there might be? I got absolutely no sense that anyone had ever stayed in this room before me.

Had he left my books here because he knew that one day I'd lose everything and be forced to come stay with him? So I could see, packed into thirty inches of shelf space, all the fruits of my labor and my life? Did he want me to ask myself, Was it worth it? Look at how small my accomplishments are. A child could carry them all away in a tiny red wagon.

On another shelf I found all of my mother's photo albums. At least two dozen of them. My brother once said he would send some to me, but he never did and I never reminded him. I took the first one down. It wasn't full of baby pictures. My mother used to keep free photos going back decades in a big box and decided one weekend to put them all into albums, in no discernible order. I flipped through the pages.

My old man watering the lawn, washing the car, sweeping the patio, reshingling the roof. His Navy tattoos could barely be seen on his forearms beneath the thick black hair. His muscles bulged and he smiled with all his hipness, a real sharp joy. My mother cooking, sitting around the table smoking at parties, wearing funny birthday hats, standing at waterfalls, on beaches, in front of Broadway theatres. My brother as a youth, on a bicycle, on a motorcycle, in a Mustang. With a blonde, a brunette, a redhead, another blonde, another brunette, even a black girl as my father stood in the background looking uncomfortably aware of his own inherent old-school racism. Me with my childhood love, at the prom, holding my diploma, at college orientation. My mother holding up my first novel with a wide smile, her eyes lit with delight. My mother holding up my second novel, looking less interested, not so happy. My mother holding up my third book, bored, faking a smile and doing a poor job of it. I remembered what she said next. "I read the bestseller lists every week, and your name is never on it." My wedding. My wife. My lips pressed to her temple, eyes closed, mouth caught in some kind of half-whisper, but I couldn't remember what I was saying. Her eyes closed too, lips tugged into the smallest of grins. We had a huge print of that picture hanging over our fireplace. When she left, I took it down and kicked it to pieces and chucked it in. Let the next family use it as kindling.

My brother opened the door and said, "What is it?"

"What?"

"I thought you called me."

"I didn't."

"I heard you say something."

"I don't think I said anything."

"I heard you."

"I was ruminating."

"It was loud."

"I ruminate loudly."

Finally, that seemed to appease him. "Oh."

"Sorry, I didn't mean to disturb you."

"You didn't. Good night."

"Night."

"Don't let the dog sleep on the bed."

He vanished down the hall. I closed the door. I turned and Church was trying his best to leap onto the bed but his stubby legs couldn't make it. I hefted him up. We crawled under my mother's half-finished blanket. He let out a low sigh of contentment as I stroked his meaty back. I shut my eyes.

gainst God and nature. Against the splintered remnant
st you, you dumbass fuck. One against me. Against all of r
nature. Against the splintered remnants of my generation.
s fuck. One against me. Against all of mankind. Against C
e splintered remnants of my generation. Against you, you c
me. Against all of mankind. Against God and nature. Aga
:s of my generation. Against you, you dumbass fuck. One aga
kind. Against God and nature. Against the splintered remnar
st you, you dumbass fuck. One against me. Against all of r
nature. Against the splintered remnants of my generation.
s fuck. One against me. Against all of mankind. Against C
e splintered remnants of my generation. Against you, you c
me. Against all of mankind. Against God and nature. Aga
:s of my generation. Against you, you dumbass fuck. One aga
kind. Against God and nature. Against the splintered remnar
st you, you dumbass fuck. One against me. Against all of r
nature. Against the splintered remnants of my generation.
s fuck. One against me. Against all of mankind. Against C
e splintered remnants of my generation. Against you, you c
me. Against all of mankind. Against God and nature. Aga
:s of my generation. Against you, you dumbass fuck. One aga
kind. Against God and nature. Against the splintered remnar
st you, you dumbass fuck. One against me. Against all of r
nature. Against the splintered remnants of my generation.
s fuck. One against me. Against all of mankind. Against C
a splintered remnants of my generation. Against you, you c
me. Against all of mankind. Against God and nature. Aga
:s of my generation. Against you, you dumbass fuck. One aga
kind. Against God and nature. Against the splintered remnar
st you, you dumbass fuck. One against me. Against all of r
nature. Against the splintered remnants of my generation.

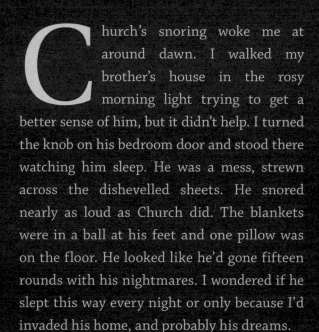

C hurch's snoring woke me at around dawn. I walked my brother's house in the rosy morning light trying to get a better sense of him, but it didn't help. I turned the knob on his bedroom door and stood there watching him sleep. He was a mess, strewn across the dishevelled sheets. He snored nearly as loud as Church did. The blankets were in a ball at his feet and one pillow was on the floor. He looked like he'd gone fifteen rounds with his nightmares. I wondered if he slept this way every night or only because I'd invaded his home, and probably his dreams.

I circled town falling back into the same Saturday night roaming pattern I'd established twenty-five years ago. North up the strip down 357, then coming around and passing the high school, the rec centre, the local community college, east to the ice cream parlour and movie theatre. I expected to be assailed by memories but only a few of them came. The places had changed too much, or maybe I'd just forgotten. Buildings had been torn down, parking lots expanded, a new science building added to the college and a security gate around the front of the high school. Two guards were posted in a small booth. I drove up to a semaphore arm and wondered how many other members of my class had come home to stare at the buses and kids and visit our old teachers in a befuddled effort to rediscover themselves.

Holding a clipboard, one of the guards poked his head out of a tiny window and asked for my ID.

"I'm just looking," I told him.

"Looking? Looking at what?"

"I don't know."

"Does your child attend this school?"

"I'm revisiting the scene of the crime."

"What crime?" he asked.

I wasn't sure. I felt like I'd been lied to, or that somehow it was me who'd told the lies that had become my life.

"Are you reporting a crime?" he said.

Yes, I almost told him. One against me. Against all of mankind. Against God and nature. Against the splintered remnants of my generation. Against you, you dumbass fuck. You work inside a three-by-three teeny booth. You're wearing a badge on your shirt but you're not a cop. You've got a nice thick leather utility belt packed with pepper spray, a nightstick, maybe a taser. When they really let you dress up they might even give you a sidearm to chase the drug-dealing tykes down the halls, just so you can practise your diving and rolling across the gym room floor.

I craned my neck and saw they had a little television in there hooked to a DVD player. They were watching an Asian action picture about a Japanese girl in her little school uniform who was actually an assassin with a machine gun in her cooch. I used to have a copy before I turned it over to the nameless pawnshop. The other security guard turned his head to glance at me. I was surprised they were watching the movie with subtitles, the only way you should ever watch a foreign flick.

"I need your ID, sir."

You always knew you'd gotten under someone's skin when they hit you with the "sir" that came across nastier than "you piece of shit." Even Churchill picked up on it. He let out a low groan. He angled his chin back and forth like he couldn't shake a buzzing insect out of his ear. I was doing the same thing. I snapped on the radio and air conditioner taking deep breaths. The music was loud and angry and aggressive. I liked it. I couldn't make out the lyrics but I could sense what the song was about. The guard kept talking at me. He put his hand on his hip like he had a holster there. He didn't. I put my hand in my pocket like I had a gun there. I did.

Yes, Officer High School Security Guard, I'd like to report a crime. Go inside and find my guidance counsellor, grab him by the collar and shake him until his back molars crack to pieces. Rap him upside the head with a dictionary. Tell him he shouldn't perpetuate the fallacy that we can all be whatever we want to be. That all we have to do to achieve it is want something badly enough and work diligently enough. Spray his eyes and watch him flail screaming across his desk. Tell him to find a new line of work. Tell him there are a lot of others coming up behind me who'll be visiting him soon. Tell him an army of his former victims is marching across the face of the earth at this very moment. Tell him I'll soon be back with a different face and a different dog in a different car, but it will be me, and I'll still have a gun in my pocket. And the next time I might just draw it, and the next time I might just pull the trigger. Yes, I want to report a crime. Someone is being murdered.

ny shoulder checking the street. She eyed me hard but I
sity there, as well as compassion and even a touch of lc
l a smile but never quite got there. She stared over my s
t. She eyed me hard but I thought I saw a little curiosity t
n and even a touch of love. Her lips almost framed a smile bt
e stared over my shoulder checking the street. She eyed n
y a little curiosity there, as well as compassion and even a t
)st framed a smile but never quite got there. She stared c
the street. She eyed me hard but I thought I saw a little c
mpassion and even a touch of love. Her lips almost framec
t there. She stared over my shoulder checking the street. S
ght I saw a little curiosity there, as well as compassion anc
ips almost framed a smile but never quite got there. She sta
ing the street. She eyed me hard but I thought I saw a little c
mpassion and even a touch of love. Her lips almost framec
t there. She stared over my shoulder checking the street. S
ght I saw a little curiosity there, as well as compassion anc
ips almost framed a smile but never quite got there. She sta
ing the street. She eyed me hard but I thought I saw a little c
mpassion and even a touch of love. Her lips almost framec
t there. She stared over my shoulder checking the street. S

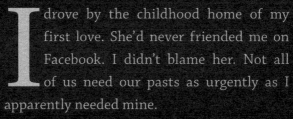

I drove by the childhood home of my first love. She'd never friended me on Facebook. I didn't blame her. Not all of us need our pasts as urgently as I apparently needed mine.

Her mother was a librarian who enjoyed recommending volumes of classic literature to me when I was a kid. Most afternoons after school I'd read there seated at a shadowed back table away from chattering students busy writing term papers or figuring out how to cheat at English exams. She'd just gotten her daughter a job at the library and the three of us would sometimes discuss novels at length, drawn together to form our own little book club. When they worked late I'd help them clear the carts and put magazines and newspapers back on the racks. They sometimes invited me out to dinner.

My childhood love and I would share ice cream sodas and platters of french fries. Her father was dead and she didn't have any siblings. I had somehow wormed my way into her life and she seemed to consider it both an amusing interlude and a slight imposition.

We shared our first kiss together, in her back yard, at fifteen. I took her to my first R-rated movie later that same year, sneaking in through a fire exit door. During the sex scenes I was horny, scared, and more than a little angry. I reached out to pet her breast and she took my wrist in a death-grip and held it in her lap. That was even worse. The heat from her belly, the nearness to her crotch, the occasional quiver whenever she laughed distracted me even worse than if I'd gotten hold of her tit.

I parked down the street and watched

the house for about an hour. The area was empty of any activity. No children played in their yards. No one tended to their lawns or gardens. I thought about how that would've gone against my old man's grain. He was always doing something for the house— sweeping the patio, weeding the flowerbeds, washing the siding. I'd felt the same way later on. I'd swept the front porch the morning the bank took my house.

I saw her mother come home and pull into the driveway. The woman had gone completely grey but somehow it looked good on her. She climbed out of the car and went around to the hatchback. She popped it open and glowered at the dozen or so bags of groceries jammed in tightly around boxes of paperbacks. She'd been slim when I'd known her twenty-five years ago but now she was stocky, thick, but with a real presence and power to her. Still, there was no way she was eating all of that food by herself. It took her four trips to carry all the groceries in. No one helped her. Then she slammed the hatchback, got back in the car, and drove away down the street.

I decided what the hell. I climbed out, crossed the lawn, knocked, and my childhood love opened the door.

She was still incredibly pretty, cute in the way you always describe the girl next door. The crows' feet and parentheses around her mouth added real character to her face. She'd kept in shape. She was trim and well-muscled, dressed nicely in tight jeans and a sleeveless blouse. There were subtle striations of colour in her brown hair, a weaving of red and blonde hues with dashes of silver. She still had a boldness in her eyes. She'd tell me to fuck off but she wouldn't lie to me.

She eyed me hard but I thought I saw a little curiosity there, as well as compassion and even a touch of love. Her lips almost framed a smile but never quite got there. She stared over my shoulder checking the street. Then she spun and glanced behind her at the hall to see if anyone was there. When she turned back to me I noticed how her hair framed her jaw line and I felt a pang for those days in tenth grade when I stared at the side of her face across our English class. I'd write typical romantic teenage angst-ridden poetry. I'd slip unsigned love haiku through the vents in her locker. It embarrassed the hell out of her.

At a party, bolstered by beer and 151 rum, I eventually found the nerve to lead her to the basement couch and flail against her. We made out, her mouth the flavour of kamikazes. I worked her pants down while she asked, "Will you still be my friend, after?" I told her I would always love her.

Her hair swept to a standstill against the fabric of her collar while she searched my face and found everything that was wrong and lacking.

"You shouldn't be here," she said.

"Why not?"

"I'm married now."

"I know that."

"I have three children."

"Congratulations."

She frowned, not sure how to take it, but accepted it as it was meant: honestly. "Thank you. You really should go."

"Why are you back living with your mother?" I asked.

"We've had some difficulties. My husband lost his job."

I nodded. I didn't know what else to do.

"He'll go berserk if he finds you here."

"Why?"

"He's very jealous."

I remembered him. He was a couple years older than us. She'd met him at a school dance he shouldn't have been at. He drove up in a well-waxed, fuel-injected red Mustang, timing his entrance perfectly for the greatest effect. The kids were all outside in line waiting to get into the rec centre. He stomped the gas about a block away so that by the time he cruised into the parking lot the engine was roaring like a jungle beast. He climbed out wearing a rat packer black suit, white shirt, black tie, his cuffs shot. They were back in style. Aloof expression, hair slick, a trimmed van dyke.

I danced with her most of the night but every time I went for punch I came back to find him talking to her. Afterwards, when I was about to drive her home, she got into his car instead. For months after I thought he would use her, break her heart, and she'd limp back to me a wiser woman ready to receive my genuine love. It never happened.

"If he doesn't have a job where's he at right now?" I asked.

"Over at the Dugout."

Christ, I thought, the Dugout. It was a hole in the wall dive where me and my buddies used to hang out Friday nights shooting pool. I could imagine her husband in there, in the middle of the day, with the place packed wall to wall with similar silent, stewing, jealous men. I would fit right in. Maybe he and I could finally be friends all these years later. He would break down and weep into three fingers of Jameson's and explain to me how life had gone downhill since that night at the rec centre. That's when he'd been at his coolest. I'd rub his shoulder and say I understood. We'd come back here and scrape together enough money to rent one of those Asian teenie bopper assassin flicks and laugh our guts out while we ate his mother-in-law's munchies.

"Let me in," I told her.

"I can't let you in."

"Just for a minute."

"Why?"

"Why do you think?"

"I have no idea."

I thought of bulling my way inside. I thought of pressing my new slim body up against hers and letting her feel the corded muscles of my chest. I could take off my jacket and show her the veins bulging in my arms. My hands were still soft but they were strong, finally. I thought I could grab her by the wrist and lead her past her three kids and tell them not to disturb us for about an hour. I'd drag her into her old bedroom. I'd never stepped foot inside it. I would stand at the edge of the doorway and glance inside while she finished brushing her hair or putting on her shoes. Her mother would hover nearby waiting to crack a vase over my head.

"You have to go now."

"Can't I just talk to you for a little while?"

"We have nothing to say to each other."

It was probably true. Besides, I didn't really want to talk to her. I wanted to haul her onto her bed and brush the hair away from her jaw line and kiss her throat gently. I wanted to work my lips in deeply and gnaw. There would be nipping. There would be biting. I'd kick the door shut and shove the dresser in front of it. I'd take off her top and maul those tits. They were still large with some nice bounce. I'd cup them and hold them up to my mouth and suck them until she whimpered. I'd tear her jeans off and shred her panties. I'd be rough. I was never rough, I wasn't aggressive, I hardly ever made the first move, not even with my wife, but

I would be rough with her. Maybe she'd want it that way, maybe not. It wouldn't matter. We'd fuck like terrified lemmings about to go over the cliff. She'd mark my chest with her nails. I'd have half-moon scars forever. Her jealous, drunken husband would bang on the door and ask in a liquor-spattered voice what the hell those weird sounds were. The kids would describe me. He'd remember. He'd throw his shoulder against the door and the lock would rattle and the dresser would dance while the mattress rocked insanely. She would scream. It would be part bliss and part cry for help. She'd be begging him for rescue and begging me as well. I'd do my best. I'd ride her across the mountaintops of hell. He would wobble into the kitchen and go through the junk drawer looking for a hammer. He wouldn't find one. He'd have to check the garage. He'd get his hand on a ball-peen but it would be too small to do any real damage. He'd take up an awl, a socket wrench, a tire iron. Finally, he'd find a huge claw hammer and run back in. The kids would be crying. He'd shout at them to shut the fuck up, you little shits. Once, twice, three times he'd strike the doorknob of the bedroom but the lock would hold. He'd kick at it, throw his hip against it. Then he'd use the hammer again. I'd be deep in his wife and nearly there as she wrapped her legs around me and told me not to stop. I wouldn't stop. I'd never stop. I would always love her. We'd come together and she'd lick at my bleeding chest, lie back and light a cigarette. The claw of the hammer would start breaking through the door. Splinters and chips would shower over us.

She'd blow a long stream of smoke that would break wide across her chin and say to me, Okay, so what do you want to talk about?

The car horn blasted. I started and jumped a little. I turned to see Churchill standing on his front paws propped against the steering wheel. His tongue lolled. He cocked his head and gave me a look like, What the hell are we doing here?

She leaned in closer. For a moment I thought she might kiss me. Her breath tickled my nose hairs. I half-closed my eyes. I waited. She whispered, "It was nice seeing you. I wish you all the best. Now please please *please* . . . don't ever come back." Then she shut the door and double locked it.

Under protest, my brother let Church stay with him while I took the train into Penn Station and walked over to my agent's office.

Of course my agent hadn't been expecting me. When I walked in he put on a false broad smile and went three shades of pale. He still had three of my novels circulating. At least he'd had them in the slush bins up until I'd had to disconnect my phone and sell my computer. He asked me how I'd been.

"Any word?" I asked.

It was a stupid question. I'd been compelled to ask it anyway. I wondered why I even cared anymore. Maybe I didn't. I could feel my time running out, and I liked the feeling. I'd had two mentors in my life and they'd both died at their desks. I wasn't going to go out that way. Their sales were still good and their royalties kept their families comfortable even now, years later. Me, I was going to die with my hands wrapped around someone's throat, maybe my own.

"No, we haven't had any offers yet," he said. "We came close with . . . ah . . . with . . ." He dipped his head trying to remember which publisher might've shown the slightest interest in my work, but he couldn't come up with it. "Anyway, they balked because they felt it wasn't commercial enough."

"Do we even know what the fuck that means?"

"It means not enough middle-age women or tween girls are going to like it."

"Is that the only audience left?"

"The only one that counts."

His phone rang and he held up a finger to shush me while he took the call.

I got out of my chair and looked through his bookcases. The same old feeling of envy began rising inside me, but it was muted this time, so deep that it couldn't seem to break the surface anymore. I saw books that were massive bestsellers yet showed no style or originality. I didn't blame the authors for writing them. I didn't even blame the readers for reading them. I plucked a novel up and flipped through some pages and found a sentence: *I was so angry I kicked him in the shin.*

I wondered how angry that might be. I wondered just how mad the author had to feel in order to kick someone in the shin. Everything was relative. Was that the culmination of his fury? Was he worse off than me? Did his wife have to leave him for a sweetie before he would kick someone in the shin?

My agent was giggling, saying, "Right right right, oh yes, yes! Yes!" It sounded like phone sex to me. He quivered in his seat. He was in love with his other clients, at least the successful ones. I still hadn't cashed my royalty cheque for $12.37.

When he finally hung up his eyes

shimmered with genuine affection. I almost asked him who he'd been talking to. But when you got down to it, I really didn't want to know.

I asked if there'd been any film interest in my novels. He just pursed his lips and shook his head. I asked if there was any other work to be found. Writing comics, being a ghost writer. Anything.

I'd asked these same questions a year ago, and six months ago, and three months ago, and six weeks ago, each time the strain of desperation growing in my voice. Now though, I was surprised to hear myself sounding quite calm. Bored even. I wondered what would have happened if he'd said there was a producer interested in turning one of my books into a movie. Would I have shouted yippee? Did I have the ability to shout yippee anymore? Had I ever?

"I've been working on a new novel," I said.

He was busy checking his daily planner and nodded without interest. "Good good. What's it about?"

"I don't want to ruin it for you. I think you should go in cold and unbiased."

I opened the rucksack, reached in, and brought out four of the full legal pads. They weren't numbered. I wasn't certain if it mattered. I put them in the order that I thought I'd written them in, and I put them on his desk.

"What's this?" he asked.

"Like I said, my new novel."

"It's not even typed."

"I don't have a laptop anymore."

"Why not?"

I knew he hadn't really been listening to me over the last year. I knew that he didn't fully grasp my situation. He didn't know my wife had left me. He wouldn't remember that my house had been taken away. He had no real idea I was homeless and destitute. He never would.

"Have your girl type it up," I told him.

"That's not her job." He glanced through the

pages. He made faces. He looked at me from time to time. "This isn't how we do things."

"No, it's not," I agreed. "I'm trying something new."

He started to argue more. Then he looked at the rucksack at my feet and his eyes opened wide and he pushed away from his desk.

"Is that a gun?" he asked.

The righteous answer would be to say, No, I'm just happy to see you. Instead I just said, "Yes."

"What are you doing with a gun?"

That was the fucking question, wasn't it? Did I tell him I wasn't sure, that I had no idea? Or did I go a little deeper with this man who had promised to do his best professionally to protect my work and make me enough money so that I could at least keep a roof over my wife's head? Had he failed me or had I failed him?

I wasn't completely mad dog yet. I wasn't going to pull the trigger on everyone who'd ever crossed me or pissed me off or written a bad review of my work. I wasn't going to put one in my own ear just so my sales might spike a little the way they did for all dead authors. Besides, who would get the royalties? I wasn't even sure. I was divorced, I was alone. I had no will or executor. I supposed the rights would go to my brother. He would look down at the paperwork, squinting, and not want to be bothered. Everything would go out of print practically overnight and in twenty years some kid with some taste might be crawling around a second hand shop or thrift store and find one of my titles in the corner of a dark shelf. He'd draw it out and turn to the first page and find the paper had been chewed on by rats and was speckled with spider eggs and fly shit.

"I don't know," I said.

"I think . . . I think maybe you should . . ."

"Don't worry, I'm not here to punch your ticket. I've been on the road for a couple of weeks and needed protection."

"Protection from what?" he asked.

It was a list that had no beginning or end. "Let's not get off point. I think you'll like the new book. I think it will move fast for us. I think it will be a big seller."

I wasn't sure how straight I was playing it. Maybe I came off as absurd as I sounded, or maybe I had more faith in those words, whatever they were, than I realized.

He decided to patronize me. He stuck a hand out as if to touch my shoulder but he never made contact. "Okay, that's good. That's a good thing. I'm glad you feel that way. If you feel that way, then it must be true. I'm sure something will break for us soon. I'll have my girl get right on it."

"Thanks."

"And I'll keep pushing the others."

"You're the man."

"Something will break. Keep the faith."

"Do my best."

"We'll get you a nice fat cheque soon."

"Terrific."

"Hollywood is always after new material."

"That's inspiring."

"This new book, I've got a good feeling about it."

"Right."

"Everything is going to turn around. We'll get you back on top."

I'd never been on top but I smiled pleasantly at him. When I picked up the rucksack he backed up to the far wall and cringed against the window. The blue sky burned around his silhouette. I wondered if I was angry enough to kick him in the shin. I wondered if I was angry enough to shoot him in the head.

The phone rang and he turned his back on me. I couldn't hold it against him. It was his training, it was instinct by now. I wasn't there anymore. Perhaps I never had been.

After a moment he started chuckling, then tittering. "Yes, yes! Right, oh right right!"

I thought of pulling the piece and putting one in his thigh. The underworld heroes of my stories often shot each other in the thick meat of their thighs. It was a way of saying that they were bad but not too bad. That they could handle violence with ease but still kept life in some kind of high regard. I put my hand in the rucksack and got my fist around the revolver. I started to sweat. His laughter made me sick to my stomach. I glanced at the bookcase and wondered which of the names on the spines of the books he was in love with at this moment.

Toppling the bookcase across his office might make a bolder statement than shooting him in the leg, but the case was bolted to the wall.

I walked out past his girl and said goodbye. She wasn't doing anything. She wasn't reading or typing or texting or checking voice mail. She was just sitting there, lost inside herself. She didn't look up. I almost kissed her.

Block after block I passed crumbling apartment buildings and steel-gated liquor stores, gun shops, bodegas, and drug rehab clinics that looked like they were pouring out tin kettles full of methadone. Block after block I passed crumbling apartment buildings and steel-gated liquor stores, gun shops, bodegas, and drug rehab clinics that looked like they were pouring out tin kettles full of methadone. Block after block I passed crumbling apartment buildings and steel-gated liquor stores, gun shops, bodegas, and drug rehab clinics that looked like they were pouring out tin kettles full of methadone. Block after block I passed crumbling apartment buildings and steel-gated liquor stores, gun shops, bodegas, and drug rehab clinics that looked like they were pouring out tin kettles full of methadone. Block after block I passed crumbling apartment buildings and steel-gated liquor stores, gun shops, bodegas, and drug rehab clinics that looked like they were pouring out tin kettles full of methadone. Block after block I passed crumbling apartment buildings and steel-gated liquor stores, gun shops, bodegas, and drug rehab clinics that looked like they were pouring out tin kettles full of methadone.

I took the B train up to the Bronx to visit a friend. He'd written a handful of novels to great acclaim, few sales, and little cash, which didn't faze him much. He had a day job as a counsellor for the Bronx Psychiatric centre. He handled drug addicts, paranoids, firebugs, chronic masturbators, bi-polars, claustrophobes, the disassociatives, the sociopaths, and the depressives.

He'd even interviewed a serial killer once, some handsome murderer who'd managed to carve up thirty-one co-eds because he had a nice smile. Their discussions went for six hours or longer at a clip, face to face in a tiny room. The killer wasn't chained or cuffed to his chair. My bud had started off taking notes, trying to learn something about the psycho, to see what happened to the guy as a kid, what made him derail, why it had gone so far. At the end of the sessions two weeks later my friend found himself doodling in his notebook, drawing little stick figures without heads.

I started in on a new legal pad and wrote the entire forty-minute ride uptown. I tried to focus on the words and actually read them before I flipped the page, but I was scrawling too fast. I could only catch a few bits and pieces.

When we got into the Bronx I felt a different kind of looming weight above the subway, as if the earth had more iron or bone meal in it. We finally reached the station, and when I came up out of the underground the sun hit me like a diamond cutter's lamp.

I hated the Bronx. It always felt like Saturday night in Beirut. I turned a corner and the brick strongholds, stone towers, and wrought-iron bars made me feel like I was a prisoner of war being dragged into the court of an enemy castle.

Block after block I passed crumbling apartment buildings and steel-gated liquor stores, gun shops, bodegas, and drug rehab clinics that looked like they were pouring out tin kettles full of methadone.

His house was a fortress with a red steel door. There wasn't half an inch of green anywhere for a square mile. No trees, lawns, not a blade of grass. Not even any house plants out on the stoops. Even the bodegas weren't selling anything green.

I had a new kind of respect for the borough. I thought, This is the way I should have done it too. You'd need mortar to get these people out of their homes. They wouldn't smile pleasantly to the bank men. They would have carried the bank men's corpses to the river wrapped in plastic and weighted them down with overdue account statements.

I pounded on the door with the side of my fist. There was no knocker or door bell. I thumped and thumped for about a minute. He was either way up high on the third floor listening to jazz CDs or he was working late at the facility. I wasn't sure if it was safe to sit on his stoop and just wait, but I didn't want to roam very far away from his place either. I kept forgetting I had a gun.

I sat back against the red door, wary, skittish, turning to face every sound. Something was alive in a nearby alley. A cat or rats were scuttling around. Maybe it was another mid-list writer rolling in garbage holding a leash of twine attached to his dog. I could almost see him there behind the bags of trash, his bloodshot eyes glaring at me.

I checked the windows above me on both sides of the street. Most of the blinds and curtains were drawn. I saw an occasional face glancing down. I pulled the rucksack into my lap. I wondered why I'd gone to see my agent. I knew it was going to go down bad. It had been even worse than expected. It was a fool's move. This road trip was making me even dumber.

The subway rumbled under the street and shook the flagstones like an earth tremor. I liked the feeling. It moved up through my legs and into my belly and chest and continued on like a death rattle out through my open mouth. I hummed along with it.

I must've fallen asleep there. The next thing I knew I was on my back on the stoop staring straight up at him. He hovered over me with the red door wide open.

He stood five three, firm and wiry, but with jowls that made you think he was chubby if you weren't paying attention. He'd been married three times, always to women who couldn't speak English. As soon as they figured out the language they cut loose and ran.

"Hey, man," I said.

"Stand up and come inside. It's a wonder you weren't butchered where you lay."

"Is that why the door is red?" I asked.

"It makes it easier to hide the rooster blood

when they have their Santeria rituals up the block. They paint all the neighbors' houses. All the neighbors they like, that is. It's a sign to the evil spirits to pass our doors by."

"Like the angel of death passing the houses of the Jews during the tenth plague, the one that had the firstborn being sacrificed."

He frowned at me. "You couldn't tell I was just kidding? Stop lying there. Come inside."

I got up. In a lot of ways his place reminded me of the house I used to have. Books and movie posters everywhere, DVDs stacked all over, boxes full of comics, the occasional action figure or some other little toy that might have helped to inspire a story.

We sat at his kitchen table. He leaned forward, enmeshed his fingers, stared at me, and said, "You've hit the wall."

"The wall hit me."

"You can stay here for as long as you like."

"Thanks, but I'm out with my brother on Long Island for the time being."

He'd met my brother at my wedding, and had already read through the thinly veiled portrait of him in my stories. "That going to work out all right?"

"For a couple of days anyway."

"And what about after that?"

"I don't know."

I was saying that a lot. It had become my mantra.

"Okay," he said, "so tell me about it."

I told him about it. I started about eighteen months back and went straight up to carrying the last of my shit into the pawn shop. I started to explain about the crank kids and the gun and speed loader and my crooked nose and the girl at the fast food window, the flood, the pie, my first love, the security guards in their little booth, all of that, but the closer I got to discussing it the heavier my chest felt. It was as if a steel band was constricting my chest, cinching tighter and tighter.

I skipped it all and went straight to my

brother, the celebrity mag, the bath, the shelf of photo albums, my old man washing the car, my mother's disappointment by the time she held up my third novel, the agent scared, the way he should be, the bolted bookcase.

Somewhere along my discourse he got up and started to brew some tea. Whenever my voice began to rise and become too shrill he'd say, "Shhh, shhhh." Once he came up behind me in my chair and began to massage my shoulders. His touch nearly made me leap up and scream.

We drank the herbal tea. I hated herbal tea. People put too much fucking faith in herbal tea, like if the Chinese knew all the mystical zen secrets of the universe then why the fuck were they still communists? I spun the cup around on the saucer a few times until he told me to swallow all of it. I swallowed all of it. There were no tea leaves in the bottom for me to read.

"You'll feel better soon."

"Tea just punches me in the bladder."

"The tea doesn't matter. I gave you some lithium."

"Lithium?" I stared into the empty cup. "You spiked the tea with lithium?"

"Yeah. Just a little. It'll help you to relax."

"No it won't." I'd studied up on anti-depressants for one of my books featuring a schizophrenic bi-polar hitman. Then again, when I got on them the first time. Then again the second time. Then again, when I couldn't afford them and wanted to know what side effects withdrawal would put me through. "It takes up to a month for treatment to become effective. And it's used in conjunction with other drugs."

"I put some Prozac and Xanax in there too."

"Christ, man, can you mix those together? You couldn't have just picked up a six-pack? How'd you get all these drugs?"

"Stole them from work," he admitted.

"Can you just drink this shit?"

"I think so."

"You think so? Oh Christ." I was so angry

I almost kicked him in the shin. "You really aren't properly trained to medicate people, are you."

He shrugged. "It can't make you feel any worse, can it?"

He had a point. My vision began to cloud and double up. I fought to keep control. I didn't know why. "You have really shit communication skills, you know that? It's why you like women who can't speak the language. So they don't notice how badly you relate to people."

"The language of love is all that two people truly need to understand each other."

"You say crap like that and you think I need the lithium?"

"You do."

My head started to lift off my shoulders. I stumbled for the couch.

"I think it's starting to hit."

"Good, just go with it."

"But I don't want to go with it. Don't you get it? I don't—"

"Shh, you're already unconscious, you stubborn asshole. Now shut up and sleep."

I glared at him and cursed at him, then I shut up and slept.

...y and finally was slick enough to slip out of her clench. I to...

be but I didn't smell like sex. The woman moaned in her sl

at sounded like Russian. I was sweating nervously and fin

p out of her clench. I took a whiff of myself. I was ripe bu

woman moaned in her sleep and said something that soun

ating nervously and finally was slick enough to slip out of he

myself. I was ripe but I didn't smell like sex. The woman mo

d something that sounded like Russian. I was sweating n

ck enough to slip out of her clench. I took a whiff of myse

mell like sex. The woman moaned in her sleep and said so

Russian. I was sweating nervously and finally was slick en

nch. I took a whiff of myself. I was ripe but I didn't smell

ed in her sleep and said something that sounded like Russi

y and finally was slick enough to slip out of her clench. I too

be but I didn't smell like sex. The woman moaned in her sl

at sounded like Russian. I was sweating nervously and fin

p out of her clench. I took a whiff of myself. I was ripe bu

woman moaned in her sleep and said something that soun

ating nervously and finally was slick enough to slip out of he

myself. I was ripe but I didn't smell like sex. The woman mo

d something that sounded like Russian. I was sweating n

ck enough to slip out of her clench. I took a whiff of myse

mell like sex. The woman moaned in her sleep and said so

Russian. I was sweating nervously and finally was slick en

nch. I took a whiff of myself. I was ripe but I didn't smell

ed in her sleep and said something that sounded like Russi

y and finally was slick enough to slip out of her clench. I too

be but I didn't smell like sex. The woman moaned in her sl

at sounded like Russian. I was sweating nervously and fin

p out of her clench. I took a whiff of myself. I was ripe bu

woman moaned in her sleep and said something that soun

ating nervously and finally was slick enough to slip out of he

myself. I was ripe but I didn't smell like sex. The woman m

d something that sounded like Russian. I was sweating n

ck enough to slip out of her clench. I took a whiff of my

I woke up in my underwear with my face pressed to the large bosom of a naked fat woman.

She smelled of stale cream and Kahlua and was gripping me so tightly that I was having trouble breathing. I huffed air like a paint sniffer and tried to extract myself. I couldn't. I tried harder.

The woman moaned in her sleep and said something that sounded like Russian. I was sweating nervously and finally was slick enough to slip out of her clench.

I took a whiff of myself. I was ripe but I didn't smell like sex. My clothes were folded in a carefully laid out pile on the floor. I got dressed and went downstairs.

My pal was sitting on the floor in front of the television, shelling pistachios and watching a martial arts flick. Tiny Asian guys were flying around on wires smacking each other silly. Every guy seemed to love this shit.

"You've been out for almost forty-eight hours," he said. "You must be starving. There's a pot of fresh chicken soup in the fridge. Get yourself some."

I did. I ate a bowl as we watched the movie, oohing and ahhing over the very cool stunts. I got myself another bowl and then a third. When I was finished I asked, "Hey, why was there a woman in the bed with me?"

"That's Katya."

"Okay. Was she there the whole two days?"

"No, she came by yesterday and we got a little drunk."

"I'm guessing she doesn't speak any English. Are you priming her to be wife number four?"

He shrugged. "She came to the US in a cargo container with twenty-four other women. But the feds hit the local Russian mob pretty hard that week and nobody picked up the shipment. The women were stuck in there for days. Half of them died. The other half, well, you think about it. She developed claustrophobia and nictophobia. She's terrified of darkness. I was her counselor. She was released from the hospital a couple days ago but had nowhere to stay, so I offered her the spare room."

"But I was in the spare room," I said.

"She's afraid of enclosed places but spent so much time in the container clutching her sister that she only sleeps well when she's holding someone."

"And the sister?" I asked.

"Dead before they got the container off the docks. Katya held onto the corpse for four or five days."

"Holy mother fuck."

He finished the pistachios and wiped his hands on a napkin. "So don't be too upset she shared a bed with you. Take it as a sign of reassurance that you're still human. That you continue to give solace, even if you're not making the effort. It was the first time in weeks she didn't wake up in the middle of the night screaming."

"Did you spike her tea?"

"She didn't need it."

"Maybe I didn't either."

"No, you definitely did," he said. Then, after a lengthy pause, "I read some of your new book."

That meant he'd been through the rucksack. That meant he'd seen the gun. He was a counsellor for the dangerous and the demented. I wondered if he'd taken the revolver away, for my own good. I half-heartedly hoped he had.

"No, you didn't," I told him. "No one can read my handwriting. Even I can't. Besides, most of it is with the agent."

"I'm used to reading the longhand scrawls of psychotics. I teach a class at the facility called Greater Self-control Through Creative Writing. You should see some of the tales they turn in."

I thought, Great, more literary competition. Maybe one of the lunatics at the hospital had been on the phone with my agent when I'd left. Maybe the next blockbuster to crush my sales was going to come out of Ward C by a guy who used to make ceramic ashtrays.

"Keep going with it," he said. "It's some of the best work you've ever done."

"It is?"

"I think so. I got choked up in a couple of spots. It's a real page-turner, thoughtful, insightful. There's a poignancy to it that's lacking in most of your other novels. You're writing from the marrow. I can feel every shallow cut you've ever suffered in it, all of them still bleeding, tearing wider and becoming deeper. You can die from a paper cut if it becomes infected. That's what I feel in your words now."

I didn't know whether to say thank you or not. I felt vaguely offended and sensed I was somehow being insulted. But his expression was sincere. And I couldn't argue about the quality of my masterpiece. Hell, I couldn't even read it.

Katya came down in a lace bathrobe, curvy and glowing, hanging out in a couple of the right places and all of the wrong ones. She grinned at me like we shared a secret. Maybe it was her way of flirting.

She said something in Russian to him. He smiled and grunted, "Uh huh." She said something more and he nodded. She started to laugh and made a vague gesture and spoke again. He mimicked the gesture and laughed loudly with her.

He didn't know a fucking word of Russian. This is how he lured his wives in. By just nodding and grinning and appearing more agreeable than any other man they'd ever met.

I grabbed my rucksack and said, "I'll leave you to your burgeoning romance."

"I think you should stay," he said. "That or let me take you over to the hospital."

"What?"

His features were empty of attitude. His

eyes were a little sad but I wasn't sure that was just for me. "You're having a nervous breakdown. You must realize it."

"Well, yeah," I admitted. "But I don't think I'm quite crazy enough to agree to being locked up in the Bronx Psychiatric Facility."

"I could call a few of the orderlies to come by in an ambulance. They'll help load you up, if you prefer."

I stepped back and wondered if he was joking or if he was even more bent than I was. "Thanks anyway."

He said, "You're going to hurt yourself or someone else very badly."

It sounded almost like a plan. We all needed plans in our lives. Schemes, agendas, ambitions, intentions. Purpose. I'd been drifting like a weather balloon lost in the clouds. I needed direction, whatever it might be. I needed a little hope that I still had a destiny to fulfill.

"Maybe that's just the next thing I have to do," I told him and shouldered my way out of

his red door that would hide dripping symbols
written in blood and allow the angel of death
to pass by.

acceptable to be a junkie or to have hit the wall and come
actically cry on the doorstep of your childhood love, who
the house? Would the cops frown on lithium, Prozac, an
heroin and crack? Was it more acceptable to be a junkie or
ome crawling back home to practically cry on the doorstep
no double-locked you out of the house? Would the cops f
d Xanax the way they did heroin and crack? Was it more ac
have hit the wall and come crawling back home to practical
ur childhood love, who double-locked you out of the house
lithium, Prozac, and Xanax the way they did heroin and cra
e to be a junkie or to have hit the wall and come crawling ba
on the doorstep of your childhood love, who double-loc
Would the cops frown on lithium, Prozac, and Xanax the w
ack? Was it more acceptable to be a junkie or to have hit
g back home to practically cry on the doorstep of your c
-locked you out of the house? Would the cops frown on
the way they did heroin and crack? Was it more acceptabl
hit the wall and come crawling back home to practically cr
childhood love, who double-locked you out of the house? W
tium, Prozac, and Xanax the way they did heroin and crack
o be a junkie or to have hit the wall and come crawling ba
on the doorstep of your childhood love, who double-loc
Would the cops frown on lithium, Prozac, and Xanax the
cr
wh
do
an

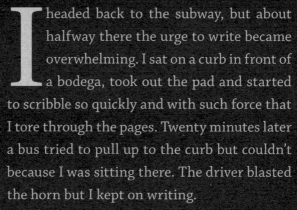

I headed back to the subway, but about halfway there the urge to write became overwhelming. I sat on a curb in front of a bodega, took out the pad and started to scribble so quickly and with such force that I tore through the pages. Twenty minutes later a bus tried to pull up to the curb but couldn't because I was sitting there. The driver blasted the horn but I kept on writing.

A cop tapped me on the shoulder with his nightstick. He was maybe twenty-five and had the doubly smug smile of someone who had both youth and power.

"Do you need some help, buddy?" he asked.

"No."

"You can't sit there. You're blocking a bus stop."

"Right. Sorry about that." I stared down at the pad and realized that I'd broken the point of the pencil off after the first couple of words. The rest was just indentations. I stuffed the pad back into my rucksack and got to my feet.

"Let me see some ID," he said.

Everyone with a badge wanted to see my ID, like they had to make sure that I was really me. I wondered, Who would want to be me if they didn't *have* to be me? I showed him my driver's license.

"Are there any issues with your license I should be aware of?"

"What?"

He repeated himself. I repeated myself. We locked gazes.

"It's a Colorado license."

"That's right."

"What are you doing in the south Bronx?"

"Visiting a friend."

"Where's he live?"

"In a big brick house with a red door a few blocks away. I don't know the address. Apparently there's a lot of Santeria worshippers around there."

"Sir, would you mind turning out your pockets?"

He tapped the license across his knuckles and the grinning face in the photo seemed to mock me. I didn't answer the cop. I looked at the photo, taken seven years ago, and wondered who the fuck that guy was and why my name was printed under the picture. The cop kept flapping the license, the face bobbing, my head pounding.

I turned out my pockets. They were empty except for my wallet and car keys.

"Have you been indulging in any alcohol or drug use?" he asked.

Would the cops frown on lithium, Prozac, and Xanax the way they did heroin and crack? Was it more acceptable to be a junkie or to have hit the wall and come crawling back home to practically cry on the doorstep of your childhood love, who double-locked you out of the house?

"I had some powerful green tea," I said.

"Are you using a euphemism for marijuana?"

"No, I am not."

"I see, sir."

I hadn't expected the police in the Bronx to be so friendly. I just figured the guy would grab my wrist and wrench my arm up my back, cuff me, and throw me in the back of the patrol car.

"Sir, what's in the bag?"

"My novel," I said. "Or a part of it anyway. My agent's girl is going to type it up. He's sure something will break for us soon. And he's going to keep pushing the other manuscripts. I'm keeping the faith. He's going to get me a nice fat cheque soon. Hollywood is always after new material. This new book, he's got a good feeling about it. Everything is going to turn around. He's going to get me back on top."

"Please open the bag, sir."

I had a feeling my rights were being violated. I wanted to beat his young, handsome face in.

Wasn't there anyone anywhere who would just let you go on your way without making you try to explain yourself? How could you articulate what you didn't understand yourself?

I smiled pleasantly. I opened the rucksack.

"Do you mind if I take a look at what you might have inside?"

"Not at all, officer."

I tossed the rucksack at his feet. He bent to examine it and realized his mistake almost instantly. I brought my knee up hard into his chin. It was my signature move now, I supposed. An ugly crunch echoed across the busy street as blood burst from his mouth. The bodega boys stopped all the buying and selling of fruit on the sidewalk and froze to the spot. I didn't want to fight a cop. I didn't want to fight anybody. I wanted to be left alone, but I couldn't even walk down a street in the south Bronx with an illegal gun packed in my bag without some bastard with his whole shitting life in front of him and the power of right and might on his side bothering me. The cop rolled and tried to reach for his gun. I nearly shut my eyes and waited for it to be over. Instead I booted him in the nuts. The gun fell out of his hand. A bus pulled up to the curb and a dozen people got off and nearly walked over the kid. I picked up my rucksack and got on the bus. The driver barked at me in Spanish and I handed him a bunch of coins. He tried to give them back and yelled louder. I pulled out a twenty and threw it at him, then went to sit. I didn't know where the bus was going and I didn't care. I haven't killed anyone yet, I thought. I stared at the back of the driver's head for miles.

him. He was hugging me. He started crying. It shocked the
ed me even worse. I broke his hold, gave him two short jab
his feet slip out from under him. He was hugging me. He
the fuckall out of me and scared me even worse. I broke h
t jabs to the nose and watched his feet slip out from under
He started crying. It shocked the fuckall out of me and sca
e his hold, gave him two short jabs to the nose and watched
him. He was hugging me. He started crying. It shocked the
ed me even worse. I broke his hold, gave him two short jab
his feet slip out from under him. He was hugging me. He
the fuckall out of me and scared me even worse. I broke h
t jabs to the nose and watched his feet slip out from under
He started crying. It shocked the fuckall out of me and sca
e his hold, gave him two short jabs to the nose and watched
him. He was hugging me. He started crying. It shocked the
ed me even worse. I broke his hold, gave him two short jab
his feet slip out from under him. He was hugging me. He
the fuckall out of me and scared me even worse. I broke h
t jabs to the nose and watched his feet slip out from under
He started crying. It shocked the fuckall out of me and sca
e his hold, gave him two short jabs to the nose and watched
him. He was hugging me. He started crying. It shocked the
ed me even worse. I broke his hold, gave him two short jab
his feet slip out from under him. He was hugging me. He
the fuckall out of me and scared me even worse. I broke
t jabs to the nose and watched his feet slip out from under
He started crying. It shocked the fuckall out of me and sca
e his hold, gave him two short jabs to the nose and watched
him. He was hugging me. He started crying. It shocked the
ed me even worse. I broke his hold, gave him two short jab
his feet slip out from under him. He was hugging me. He
the fuckall out of me and scared me even worse. I broke

It took me six hours to get back to Penn Station. The whole day was a blur of bus transfers and trains heading in the wrong direction. I finally figured out the way to get back home, caught the L.I.R.R. out of Penn and made it back to my brother's house. I rushed up his driveway and threw the rucksack in the back of my car. There wasn't any reason to go back inside except to get Church.

I walked in and my brother slid the ottoman out from under his feet and jumped out of his chair.

He hissed, "Where've you been? You've been gone for almost three whole days!"

"I had to see my agent," I said. "I had a manuscript to drop off. His girl is going to type it up. He's sure something will break for us soon. And he's going to keep pushing the other books. I'm keeping the faith. He's going to get me a nice fat cheque—"

"I had to take care of your dog. That's not my responsibility."

"Thank you. Where is he?"

My brother had the temerity to look a little self-satisfied. "In the garage."

I glared at him. "You piece of shit."

I went to the kitchen and through the door to the garage. Church was tied to a nail hammered into a work bench, sitting, waiting, looking a bit stunned. There was a bucket of water and an open can of tuna fish in front of him. When he looked at me he got to his feet and his ass started swaying. He groaned out a little yelp.

I untied him and pulled him into my arms and buried my face in the folds of his chest fat. I hugged him and after a while I began to whimper, *"I'm sorry I'm sorry I'm so sorry, Church, I'm sorry I'm sorry . . ."*

The worst thing that had ever happened to my dog had been me finding him in that cage in the pet store. If I had just moved along he'd be settled in with some loving family, an attentive and adoring mommy and daddy, and a little girl that hadn't been scraped out of a womb. He'd be chasing tennis balls around the yard and eating barbecue all summer long, stretched out on a patio deck.

"I'm so sorry, Church, I'm sorry I'm so sorry . . ."

"What's happened?" my brother cried. "What's going on with you?"

I gritted my teeth. I fought for air. "I'm leaving."

"What? Leaving? Why?" He tried to pull Church out my arms and both me and the dog growled at him. "Why are you doing this?"

I found the button to open the garage door and hit it with my elbow. Then I ran to my car carrying my dog with my brother on my heels.

"Where are you going?"

"Away."

"I don't understand."

"Neither do I!"

I flung open the driver's door and tossed Churchill in. He climbed across to the passenger seat and got his front paws up on the dashboard, staring at me. I started to get in and my brother grabbed my arm.

"Don't," he said. "Stay here."

"There's no point."

"I want you to."

"That's not a good enough reason."

"I've liked having you around. You and the dog."

"Now you're just flat-out lying."

"No, I'm not. Besides—" His hard face began to crumble. I watched as it softened up around the edges and began to fall in. "There are things I should tell you. That I want to tell you."

"I don't want to hear," I said. "Keep your secrets. Everyone has them. I'm not telling you mine."

"I don't need to hear yours if you don't want to share." He shook his head. We had jumped the tracks again. He pulled us back on topic. "The point is you're my brother. I love you."

"Oh Christ, don't. Don't say it."

"I can take care of you."

"Don't you understand that just makes it worse?"

"Let me help you."

"You can't!" I reached into the rucksack, pulled out the revolver, and pointed it at my brother's chest.

His hands flashed up to protect himself. "Christ, what are you doing with that!"

"I don't know."

"Stop it. Stop pointing it at me."

I lowered the gun.

"What's this?" he asked. "What's this mean?"

"I don't know."

"You're going to get yourself into bad trouble."

"I'm already in bad trouble."

"What did you do?"

I didn't know. I didn't know what I'd done or where I'd gone wrong or how to fix it. I wasn't sure what the next step should be, where I should go, how I could lift myself out. I wanted to go home. I didn't have a home to go to. I wanted to finish the new book. I wondered what the ending would be. I wanted to tell my mother, There's my name, Ma, right there on the bestseller list. I wanted to add new photos to the old photo albums.

I shouldered past my brother.

"Wait," he said. He reached out to grab hold of me in his powerful arms. He was hugging me. He started crying. It shocked the fuckall out of me and scared me even worse. I broke his hold, gave him two short jabs to the nose and watched his feet slip out from under him. He clutched at his face.

"Don't you get it?" I said. "If I stay here any longer I'm going to shoot you in the fucking head."

thought this should be easy by now. I thought this should
this should be easy by now. I thought this should be easy b
d be easy by now. I thought this should be easy by now. I
by now. I thought this should be easy by now. I thought thi
thought this should be easy by now. I thought this should
this should be easy by now. I thought this should be easy b
d be easy by now. I thought this should be easy by now. I
by now. I thought this should be easy by now. I thought thi
thought this should be easy by now. I thought this should
this should be easy by now. I thought this should be easy b
d be easy by now. I thought this should be easy by now. I
by now. I thought this should be easy by now. I thought thi
thought this should be easy by now. I thought this should
this should be easy by now. I thought this should be easy b
d be easy by now. I thought this should be easy by now. I
by now. I thought this should be easy by now. I thought thi
thought this should be easy by now. I thought this should
this should be easy by now. I thought this should be easy b
d be easy by now. I thought this should be easy by now. I
by now. I thought this should be easy by now. I thought thi
thought this should be easy by now. I thought this should
this should be easy by now. I thought this should be easy b
d be easy by now. I thought this should be easy by now. I
by now. I thought this should be easy by now. I thought thi
thought this should be easy by now. I thought this should
this should be easy by now. I thought this should be easy b
d be easy by now. I thought this should be easy by now. I
by now. I thought this should be easy by now. I thought thi
thought this should be easy by now. I thought this should
this should be easy by now. I thought this should be easy b
d be easy by now. I thought this should be easy by now. I
by now. I thought this should be easy by now. I thought thi
thought this should be easy by now. I thought this should

I got behind the wheel and started the car. It was almost out of gas. What the hell. I jacked it into reverse with the tires squealing, pulled out of my brother's driveway, and then wheeled off screeching down the road as he staggered after us. I kept my eyes on the rearview watching him become smaller and smaller until he was nothing. I stood on the pedal and the engine screamed. I got on a highway I didn't recognize and jockeyed through traffic heading nowhere. Eventually I put the gun to Churchill's head and pressed the muzzle between his eyes. He stared at me with that same puzzled expression. This is what they did before they took themselves out. They iced their wives and children. Gave them poisoned punch or put a bullet in their hearts. It was an act of benevolence and grace and kindness. You couldn't protect your loved ones but you also couldn't bear the thought of them suffering on without you. I cocked the hammer. He grunted and let his tongue hang out. His bulging fat furrowed brow swallowed two inches of the gun barrel. I loved my dog. I pulled the revolver away and pressed it to my own temple. Maybe I'd pop myself as soon as the car stalled. Or we hit a red light. Or before we took the next exit. Or after we crossed the median into oncoming traffic. I pressed harder. I thought this should be easy by now. Church barked happily. I wasn't afraid. I knew what questions God would have waiting for me as all his legions of archangels surrounded my soul with their fiery swords, wings spattered with blood. I figured I could fudge the answers.

ABOUT THE AUTHOR

Tom Piccirilli is the author of more than twenty novels, including *Shadow Season*, *The Cold Spot*, *The Coldest Mile*, and *A Choir of Ill Children*. He's won two International Thriller Awards and four Bram Stoker Awards, as well as having been nominated for the Edgar, the World Fantasy Award, the Macavity, and Le Grand Prix de L'imagination.

Learn more at: www.thecoldspot.blogspot.com.

978-0-9812978-9-7

TIM LEBBON

THE THIEF OF BROKEN TOYS

978-0-9812978-8-0

PHILIP NUTMAN

CITIES OF NIGHT

978-0-9812978-7-3

SIMON LOGAN

KATJA FROM THE PUNK BAND

978-0-9812978-6-6

GEMMA FILES

A BOOK OF TONGUES

978-0-9812978-5-9

DOUGLAS SMITH

CHIMERASCOPE

978-0-9812978-4-2

NICHOLAS KAUFMANN

CHASING THE DRAGON

3

NAPIER'S BONES DERRYL MURPHY

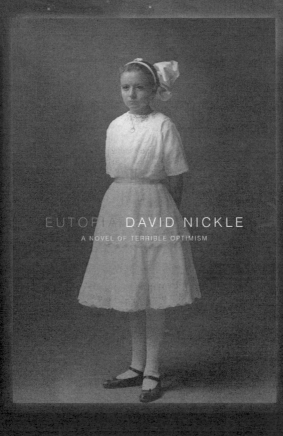

EUTOPIA DAVID NICKLE

A NOVEL OF TERRIBLE OPTIMISM

COMING APRIL 15, 2011
FROM CHIZINE PUBLICATIONS

978-1-926851-11-2

THE DOOR TO
LOST PAGES
CLAUDE LALUMIÈRE

COMING APRIL 15, 2011
FROM CHIZINE PUBLICATIONS

978-1-926851-12-9